Nan Sherwood At Pine Camp

Or, The Old Lumberman's Secret

by

Annie Roe Carr

Double 9 Books

Nan Sherwood At Pine Camp
Or, The Old Lumberman's Secret
by Annie Roe Carr

ISBN: 978-93-63053-95-3

Published by

DOUBLE 9 BOOKS
2/13-B, Ansari Road
Daryaganj, New Delhi – 110002
info@double9books.com
www.double9books.com
Tel. 011-40042856

ABOUT THE AUTHOR

Annie Roe Carr, a prolific writer, crafted a captivating masterpiece titled "Nan Sherwood at Rose Ranch: Or, The Old Mexican's Treasure." Set amidst the rugged landscapes of Rose Ranch, Carr's novel chronicles the adventures of Nan Sherwood as she embarks on a thrilling quest for treasure. With Carr's signature blend of vivid storytelling and rich character development, readers are transported to a world where mystery and intrigue collide with the beauty of the American Southwest. Through Nan's journey, Carr deftly explores themes of friendship, courage, and the enduring spirit of adventure. As Nan and her companions navigate the challenges of treasure hunting and uncover long-buried secrets, they discover the true treasures of friendship and loyalty along the way. "Nan Sherwood at Rose Ranch: Or, The Old Mexican's Treasure" stands as a testament to Carr's literary prowess and her ability to weave tales that capture the imagination and inspire readers of all ages.

CONTENTS

CHAPTER I
THE YELLOW POSTER

"Oh, look there, Nan!" cried Bess Harley suddenly, as they turned into High Street from the avenue on which Tillbury's high school was situated.

"Look where?" queried Nan Sherwood promptly. "Up in the air, down on the ground or all around?" and she carried out her speech in action, finally spinning about on one foot in a manner to shock the more staid Elizabeth.

"Oh, Nan!"

"Oh, Bess!" mocked her friend.

She was a rosy-cheeked, brown-eyed girl, with fly-away hair, a blue tam-o'-shanter set jauntily upon it, and a strong, plump body that she had great difficulty in keeping still enough in school to satisfy her teachers.

"Do behave, Nan," begged Bess. "We're on the public street."

"How awful!" proclaimed Nan Sherwood, making big eyes at her chum. "Why folks know we're only high-school girls, so, of course, we're crazy! Otherwise we wouldn't BE high-school girls."

"Nonsense!" cried Bess, interrupting. "Do be reasonable, Nan. And look yonder! What do you suppose that crowd is at the big gate of the Atwater Mills?"

Nan Sherwood's merry face instantly clouded. She was not at all a thoughtless girl, although she was of a sanguine, cheerful temperament.

The startled change in her face amazed Bess.

"Oh dear!" the latter cried. "What is it? Surely, there's nobody hurt in the mills? Your father———"

"I'm afraid, Bess dear, that it means there are a great many hurt in the mills."

"Oh, Nan! How horridly you talk," cried Bess. "That is impossible."

"Not hurt in the machinery, not mangled by the looms," Nan went on to say, gravely. "But dreadfully hurt nevertheless, Bess. Father has been expecting it, I believe. Let's go and read the poster."

"Why it is a poster, isn't it?" cried Bess. "What does it say?"

The two school girls, both neatly dressed and carrying their bags of text books, pushed into the group before the yellow quarter-sheet poster pasted on the fence.

The appearance of Nan and Bess was distinctly to their advantage when compared with that of the women and girls who made up the most of the crowd interested in the black print upon the poster.

The majority of these whispering, staring people were foreigners. All bore marks of hard work and poverty. The hands of even the girls in the group were red and cracked. It was sharp winter weather, but none wore gloves.

If they wore a head-covering at all, it was a shawl gathered at the throat by the clutch of frost-bitten fingers. There was snow on the ground; but few wore overshoes.

They crowded away from the two well-dressed high-school girls, looking at them askance. Bess Harley scarcely noticed the mill-hands' wives and daughters. She came of a family who considered these poor people little better than cattle. Nan Sherwood was so much interested in the poster that she saw nothing else. It read:

NOTICE: Two weeks from date all departments of these mills will be closed until further notice. Final payment of wages due will be made on January 15th. Over-supply of our market and the prohibitive price of cotton make this action a necessity. ATWATER MILLS COMPANY. December 28th.

"Why, dear me!" murmured Bess. "I thought it might really be something terrible. Come on, Nan. It's only a notice of a vacation. I guess most of them will be glad to rest awhile."

"And who is going to pay for their bread and butter while the poor creatures are resting?" asked Nan seriously, as the two girls moved away from the group before the yellow poster.

"Dear me, Nan!" her chum cried. "You do always think of the most dreadful things. It troubles me to know anything about poverty and poor people. I can't help them, and I don't want to know anything about them."

"If I didn't know that you are better than your talk, Bess," said Nan, still gravely, "I'd think you a most callous person. You just don't understand.

These poor people have been fearing this shut-down for months. And all the time they have been expecting it they have been helpless to avert it and unable to prepare for it."

"They might have saved some of their wages, I suppose," said Bess. "I heard father say the other night how much money the mills paid out in a year to the hands, some perfectly en*or*mous sum."

"But just think how many people that has to be divided among," urged Nan. "Lots of the men earn only eight or nine dollars a week, and have families to support."

"Well, of course, they don't have to be supported as we are," objected the easy-minded Bess. "Anyway my father says frugality should be taught to the poor just the same as reading and writing. They ought to learn how to save."

"When you earn only just enough to supply your needs, and no more, how can you divide your income so as to hoard up any part of it?"

"Dear me! Don't ask questions in political economy out of school, Nan!" cried Bess, forgetting that she had started the discussion herself. "I just HATE that study, and wish we didn't have to take it! I can't answer that question, anyway."

"I'll answer it then," declared Nan. "If you are a mill-hand your stomach won't let you save money. There probably won't be a dozen families affected by this shut-down who have more than ten dollars saved."

"Goodness! You don't mean that that's true? Why, dad gives me that much to spend on myself each month," Bess cried. "The poor things! Even if they are frowsy and low, I am sorry for them. But, of course, the shut-down doesn't trouble you, Nan. Not personally, I mean. Your father has had a good position for so many years— —-"

"I'm not at all sure that it won't trouble us," Nan interposed gravely. "But of course we are not in danger of starvation."

She felt some delicacy about entirely confiding in Bess on the subject. Nan had heard the pros and cons of the expected closing of the mills discussed at home almost every day for weeks past; but family secrets should never be mentioned outside the family circle, as Nan very well knew.

"Well," signed Bess, whose whole universe revolved around a central sun called Self, as is the case with many girls brought up by indulgent parents. "I hope, dear, that this trouble won't keep you from entering Lakeview with me next fall."

Nan laughed. "There never was a chance of my going with you, Bess, and I've told you so often enough— —-"

"Now, don't you say that, Nan Sherwood!" cried her chum. "I've just made up my mind that you shall go, and that's all there is to it! You've just got to go!"

"You mean to kidnap me and bear me off to that ogre's castle, whether or not?"

"It's the very nicest school that ever was," cried Bess. "And such a romantic place."

"Romantic?" repeated Nan curiously.

"Yes, indeed! A great big stone castle overlooking Lake Michigan, a regular fortress, they say. It was built years ago by Colonel Gilpatrick French, when he came over from Europe with some adventurous Irishmen who thought all they had to do was to sail over to Canada and the whole country would be theirs for the taking."

"Goodness me! I've read something about that," said Nan, interested.

"Well, Lakeview Hall, as the school is called, was built by that rich Colonel French. And they say there are dungeons under it."

"Where they keep their jams and preserves, now, I suppose?" laughed Nan.

"And secret passages down to the shore of the lake. And the great hall where the brave Irishmen used to drill is now the assembly hall of the school."

"Sounds awfully interesting," admitted Nan.

"And Dr. Beulah Prescott, who governs the hall, the preceptress, you know, is really a very lovely lady, my mother says," went on the enthusiastic Bess. "MY mother went to school to her at Ferncliffe."

"Oh, Bess," Nan said warmly, "It must be a perfectly lovely place! But I know I can never go there."

"Don't you say that! Don't you say that!" cried the other girl. "I won't listen to you! You've just got to go!"

"I'm afraid you'll have to kidnap me, then," repeated Nan, with a rueful smile. "I'm very sure that my father won't be able to afford it, especially now that the mills will close."

"Oh, Nan! I think you're too mean," wailed her friend. "It's my pet project. You know, I've always said we should go to preparatory school together, and then to college."

Nan's eyes sparkled; but she shook her head.

"We sat together in primary school, and we've always been in the same grade through grammar and into high," went on Bess, who was really very faithful in her friendships. "It would just break my heart, Nan, if we were to be separated now."

Nan put her arm about her. They had reached the corner by Bess's big house where they usually separated after school.

"Don't you cry, honey!" Nan begged her chum. "You'll find lots of nice girls at that Lakeview school, I am sure. I'd dearly love to go with you, but you might as well understand right now, dear, that my folks are poor."

"Poor!" gasped Bess.

"Too poor to send me to Lakeview," Nan went on steadily. "And with the mills closing as they are, we shall be poorer still. I may have to get a certificate as Bertha Pike did, and go to work. So you mustn't think any more about my going to that beautiful school with you."

"Stop! I won't listen to you another moment, Nan Sherwood!" cried Bess, and sticking her fingers in her ears, she ran angrily away and up the walk to the front door.

Nan walked briskly away toward Amity Street. She did not turn back to wave her hand as usual at the top of the hill.

CHAPTER II
THE COTTAGE ON AMITY STREET

The little shingled cottage stood back from the street, in a deeper yard than most of its neighbors. It was built the year Nan was born, so the roses, the honeysuckle, and the clematis had become of stalwart growth and quite shaded the front and side porches.

The front steps had begun to sag a little; but Mr. Sherwood had blocked them up. The front fence had got out of alignment, and the same able mechanic had righted it and set the necessary new posts.

The trim of the little cottage on Amity Street had been painted twice within Nan's remembrance; each time her father had done the work in his spare time.

Now, with snow on the ground and frozen turf peeping out from under the half-melted and yellowed drifts, the Sherwood cottage was not so attractive as in summer. Yet it was a cozy looking house with the early lamplight shining through the kitchen window and across the porch as Nan approached, swinging her schoolbooks.

Papa Sherwood called it, with that funny little quirk in the corner of his mouth, "a dwelling in amity, more precious than jewels or fine gold."

And it was just that. Nan had had experience enough in the houses of her school friends to know that none of them were homes like her own.

All was amity, all was harmony, in the little shingled cottage on this short by-street of Tillbury.

It was no grave and solemn place where the natural outburst of childish spirits was frowned upon, or one had to sit "stiff and starched" upon stools of penitence.

No, indeed! Nan had romped and played in and about the cottage all her life. She had been, in fact, of rather a boisterous temperament until lately.

Her mother's influence was always quieting, and not only with her little daughter. Mrs. Sherwood's voice was low, and with a dear drawl in it, so Nan declared.

She had come from the South to Northern Illinois, from Tennessee, to be exact, where Mr. Sherwood had met and married her. She had grace and gentleness without the languor that often accompanies those qualities.

Her influence upon both her daughter and her husband was marked. They deferred to her, made much of her, shielded her in every way possible from all that was rude or unpleasant.

Yet Mrs. Sherwood was a perfectly capable and practical housekeeper, and when her health would allow it she did all the work of the little family herself. Just now she was having what she smilingly called "one of her lazy spells," and old Mrs. Joyce came in to do the washing and cleaning each week.

It was one of Mrs. Sherwood's many virtues that she bore with a smile recurrent bodily ills that had made her a semi-invalid since Nan was a very little girl. But in seeking medical aid for these ills, much of the earnings of the head of the household had been spent.

The teakettle was singing when Nan entered the "dwelling in amity", and her mother's low rocker was drawn close to the side-table on which the lamp stood beside the basket of mending.

Although Mrs. Sherwood could not at present do her own laundry-work, she insisted upon darning and patching and mending as only she could darn and patch and mend.

Mr. Sherwood insisted that a sock always felt more comfortable on his foot after "Momsey" had darned it than when it was new. And surely she was a very excellent needlewoman.

This evening, however, her work had fallen into her lap with an idle needle sticking in it. She had been resting her head upon her hand and her elbow on the table when Nan came in. But she spoke in her usual bright way to the girl as the latter first of all kissed her and then put away her books and outer clothing.

"What is the good word from out of doors, honey?" she asked.

Nan's face was rather serious and she could not coax her usual smile into being. Her last words with Bess Harley had savored of a misunderstanding, and Nan was not of a quarrelsome disposition.

"I'm afraid there isn't any real good word to be brought from outside tonight, Momsey," she confessed, coming back to stand by her mother's chair.

"Can that be possible, Daughter!" said Mrs. Sherwood, with her low, caressing laugh. "Has the whole world gone wrong?"

"Well, I missed in two recitations and have extras to make up, in the first place," rejoined Nan ruefully.

"And what else?"

"Well, Bess and I didn't have exactly a falling out; but I couldn't help offending her in one thing. That's the second trouble."

"And is there a 'thirdly,' my dear?" queried little Mrs. Sherwood tranquilly.

"Oh, dear, yes! The worst of all!" cried Nan. "The yellow poster is up at the mills."

"The yellow poster?" repeated her mother doubtfully, not at first understanding the significance of her daughter's statement.

"Yes. You know. When there's anything bad to announce to the hands the Atwater Company uses yellow posters, like a small-pox, or typhoid warning. The horrid thing! The mills shut down in two weeks, Momsey, and no knowing when they will open again."

"Oh, my dear!" was the little woman's involuntary tribute to the seriousness of the announcement.

In a moment she was again her usual bright self. She drew Nan closer to her and her own brown eyes, the full counterpart of her daughter's, winkled merrily.

"I tell you what let's do, Nan," she said.

"What shall we do, Momsey?" repeated the girl, rather lugubriously.

"Why, let's not let Papa Sherwood know about it, it will make him feel so bad."

Nan began to giggle at that. She knew what her mother meant. Of course, Mr. Sherwood, being at the head of one of the mill departments, would know all about the announcement of the shut-down; but they would keep up the fiction that they did not know it by being particularly cheerful when he came home from work.

So Nan giggled and swallowed back her sobs. Surely, if Momsey could present a cheerful face to this family calamity, she could!

The girl ran her slim fingers into the thick mane of her mother's coiled hair, glossy brown hair through which only a few threads of white were speckled.

"Your head feels hot, Momsey," she said anxiously. "Does it ache?"

"A wee bit, honey," confessed Mrs. Sherwood.

"Let me take the pins out and rub your poor head, dear," said Nan. "You know, I'm a famous 'massagist.' Come do, dear."

"If you like, honey."

Thus it was that, a little later, when Mr. Sherwood came home with feet that dragged more than usual on this evening, he opened the door upon a very beautiful picture indeed.

His wife's hair was "a glory of womanhood," for it made a tent all about her, falling quite to the floor as she sat in her low chair. Out of this canopy she looked up at the brawny, serious man, roguishly.

"Am I not a lazy, luxurious person, Papa Sherwood?" she demanded. "Nan is becoming a practical maid, and I presume I put upon the child dreadfully, she is good-natured, like you, Robert."

"Aye, I know our Nan gets all her good qualities from me, Jessie," said her husband. "If she favored you she would, of course, be a very hateful child."

He kissed his wife tenderly. As Nan said, he always "cleaned up" at the mills and "came home kissable."

"I ought to be just next door to an angel, if I absorbed the virtues of both my parents," declared Nan briskly, beginning to braid the wonderful hair which she had already brushed. "I often think of that."

Her father poked her tentatively under the shoulder blades with a blunt forefinger, making her squirm.

"I don't feel the wings sprouting yet, Nancy," he said, in his dry way.

"I hope not, yet!" exclaimed the girl. "I'd have to have a new winter coat if you did, and I know we can't afford that just now."

"You never said a truer word, Nan," replied Mr. Sherwood, his voice dropping to a less cheerful level, as he went away to change his coat and light the hanging lamp in the dining room where the supper table was already set.

Mother and daughter looked at each other rather ruefully.

"Oh, dear me!" whispered Nan. "I never do open my mouth but I put my foot in it!"

"Goodness!" returned her mother, much amused. "That is an acrobatic feat that I never believed you capable of, honey."

"We-ell! I reminded Papa Sherwood of our hard luck instead of being bright and cheerful like you."

"We will give him a nice supper, honey, and make him forget his troubles. Time enough to call to order the ways and means committee afterward." Her husband came back into the kitchen as Nan finished arranging the hair. "Come, Papa Sherwood!" cried the little lady. "Hot biscuit; the last of the honey; sweet pickles; sliced cold ham; and a beautiful big plum cake that our Nan made this morning before school time, her own self. You MUST smile at all those dainties."

And the husband and father smiled. They all made an effort to help each other. But they knew that with the loss of his work would doubtless come the loss of the home. During the years that had elapsed, Mr. Sherwood had paid in part for the cottage; but now the property was deteriorating instead of advancing in value. He could not increase the mortgage upon it. Prompt payment of interest half-yearly was demanded. And how could he meet these payments, not counting living expenses, when his income was entirely cut off?

Mr. Sherwood was forty-five years old, an age at which it is difficult for a man to take up a new trade, or to obtain new employment at his old one.

CHAPTER III
"FISHING"

Nan told of Bess Harley's desire to have her chum accompany her to Lakeview Hall the following autumn, as a good joke.

"I hope I'll be in some good situation by that time," she said to her mother, confidentially, "helping, at least, to support myself instead of being a burden upon father and you."

"It's very unselfish of you to propose that, honey," replied her mother. "But, perhaps, such a sacrifice as the curtailment of your education will not be required of you."

"But, my DEAR!" gasped Nan. "I couldn't go to Lakeview Hall. It would cost, why! a pile!"

"I don't know how much a pile is, translated into coin of the realm, honey," responded Mrs. Sherwood with her low, sweet laugh. "But the only thing we can give our dear daughter, your father and I, is an education. That you MUST have to enable you to support yourself properly when your father can do no more for you."

"But I s'pose I've already had as much education as most girls in Tillbury get. So many of them go into the mills and factories at my age. If they can get along, I suppose I can."

"Hush!" begged her mother quickly. "Don't speak of such a thing. I couldn't bear to have you obliged to undertake your own support in any such way.

"Both your father and I, honey, had the benefit of more than the ordinary common-school education. I went three years to the Tennessee Training College; I was prepared to teach when your father and I met and married. He obtained an excellent training for his business in a technical college. We hoped to give our children, if we were blessed with them, an even better start in life than we had.

"Had your little brother lived, honey," added Mrs. Sherwood tenderly, "we should have tried to put him through college, and you, as well. It would have been something worthwhile for your father to work for. But I am afraid all these years that his money has been wasted in attempts to benefit my health."

"Oh, Momsey! Don't say it, that way," urged Nan. "What would we ever do without you? But I sometimes think how nice it would be had I been a boy, my own brother, for instance. A boy can be so much more help than a girl."

"For shame!" cried her mother, laughing. "Do you dare admit a boy is smarter than a girl, Nan?"

"Not smarter. Only better able to do any kind of work, I guess. They wouldn't let me work in the file shop, or drive a grocery wagon."

"Goodness! Listen to the child!" gasped Mrs. Sherwood. "I should hope not! Why, honey, is your mind running continually on such dreadful things? I am afraid your father and I allow you to hear us talk too frequently about family matters. You must not assume the family's burdens at your age."

There was that trend to Nan Sherwood's character, however. With all her blithesomeness and high spirits she was inclined to be serious in thought.

This conversation occurred several days after the evening when, on their way home from school, Nan and her school chum, Bess Harley, had read the yellow poster at the gate of the Atwater Mills.

The district surrounding the mills, in which most of the hands lived, had put on an aspect of mourning. Some of the workmen and their families had already packed up and gone. Most of the houses occupied by the hands were owned by the Atwater Company, and if the poor people remained till January 15th, the wages due them then would be eaten up by the rent of the tenements.

So they were wise to leave when they could. Many who remained would be a burden upon the taxpayers of Tillbury before the winter was over.

Nan and her folks were not in such a sad situation as the laborers, of course. Mr. Sherwood had a small sum in bank. He had, too, a certain standing in the community and a line of credit at the stores that he might have used.

Debt, however, save that upon their house, he had fought to keep out of all his married life. That his equity in the Amity Street cottage was so small was not his fault; but he owed not any man.

"Now we must go fishing," Mrs. Sherwood said, in her sprightly way, when the little family really discussed the unfortunate situation after the announcement of the shut-down of the mills was made public.

"Goodness, Momsey! What a reckless creature you are," laughed Mr. Sherwood. "Waste our precious time in such employment, and in the dead of winter, too?"

"Now, Papa Sherwood, I don't mean that kind of fishing at all!" cried the little woman gaily. "We are going to fish for employment for you, perhaps for a new home."

"Oh!" gasped Nan. The thought of deserting the little cottage on Amity Street was a dreadful shock.

"We must face that possibility," said her mother firmly. "It may be. Tillbury will see very hard times now that the mills are closed. Other mills and shops will follow suit."

"Quite true, Momsey," agreed the husband and father.

"I am a very logical person, am I not?" said the smiling little lady.

"But the fishing?" cried Nan curiously.

"Ah, yes. I am coming to that," said her mother. "The fishing, to be sure! Why, we are going to write letters to just everybody we know, and some we only know by hearsay, and find out if there isn't a niche for Papa Sherwood somewhere outside Tillbury."

"So we can!" cried Nan, clapping her hands.

"I am afraid there is general depression in my line of business everywhere," suggested Mr. Sherwood. "For some years the manufacturers have been forcing cotton goods upon a false market. And the recent attempt to help the cotton growers by boosting the price of raw cotton will come near to ruining the mills and mill workers. It is always so. In an attempt to benefit one class of the people another class is injured."

"Now, never mind politics, sir!" cried his little wife. "We poor, weak women aren't supposed to understand such things. Only when Nan and I get the vote, and all the other millions of women and girls, we will have no class legislation. 'The greatest good for the greatest number' will be our motto."

Mr. Sherwood only smiled. He might have pointed out that in that very statement was the root of all class legislation. He knew his wife's particular ideas were good, however, her general political panacea was rather doubtful. He listened thoughtfully as she went on:

"Yes, we must fish for a new position for papa. We may have to go away from here. Perhaps rent the house. You know, we have had good offers for it."

"True," admitted Mr. Sherwood.

"Oh, dear!" sighed Nan, but below her breath so that Momsey and Papa Sherwood did not hear the sigh.

"I am going to write to Cousin Adair MacKenzie, in Memphis. He is quite prominent in business there," pursued Mrs. Sherwood. "We might find a footing in Memphis."

Mr. Sherwood looked grave, but said nothing. He knew that the enervating climate of the Southern river city would never do for his wife. Change of climate might benefit her greatly; the doctors had all said so of late; but not that change.

"Then," continued Nan's mother, "there is your brother, Henry, up in Michigan."

"Oh! I remember Uncle Henry," cried Nan. "Such a big, big man!"

"With a heart quite in keeping with the size of his body, honey," her mother quickly added. "And your Aunt Kate is a very nice woman. Your uncle has lumber interests. He might find something for your father there."

"I'll write to Hen, Jessie," Mr. Sherwood said decisively. "But a lumber camp is no place for you. Let's see, his mail address is Hobart Forks, isn't it? Right in the heart of the woods. If you weren't eaten up by black gnats, you would be by ennui," and he chuckled.

"Goodness!" cried Mrs. Sherwood, making big eyes at him. "Are those a new kind of mosquito? Ennui, indeed! Am I a baby? Is Nan another?"

"But think of Nan's education, my dear," suggested Mr. Sherwood.

"I ought to work and help the family instead of going to school any longer," Nan declared.

"Not yet, Daughter, not yet," her father said quickly. "However, I will write to Hen. He may be able to suggest something."

"It might be fun living in the woods," Nan said. "I'm not afraid of gnats, or mosquitoes, or, or on-wees!"

She chanced to overhear her father and Dr. Christian talking the next day on the porch, and heard the wise old physician say:

"I'm not sure I could countenance that, Robert. What Jessie needs is an invigorating, bracing atmosphere. A sea voyage would do her the greatest possible good."

"Perhaps a trip to Buffalo, down the lakes?"

"No, no! That's merely an old woman's home-made plaster on the wound. Something more drastic. Salt air. A long, slow voyage, overseas. It often wracks the system, but it brings the patient to better and more stable health. Jessie may yet be a strong, well woman if we take the right course with her."

Nevertheless, Mr. Sherwood wrote to his brother. He had to do so, it seemed. There was no other course open to him.

And while he fished in that direction, Momsey threw out her line toward Memphis and Adair MacKenzie. Mr. Sherwood pulled in his line first, without much of a nibble, it must be confessed.

"Dear Bob," the elder Sherwood wrote: "Things are flatter than a stepped-on pancake with me. I've got a bunch of trouble with old Ged Raffer and may have to go into court with him. Am not cutting a stick of timber. But you and Jessie and the little nipper," ("Consider!" interjected Nan, "calling me 'a little nipper'! What does he consider a big 'nipper'?") "come up to Pine Camp. Kate and I will be mighty glad to have you here. Tom and Rafe are working for a luckier lumberman than I, and there's plenty of room here for all hands, and a hearty welcome for you and yours as long as there's a shot in the locker."

"That's just like Hen," Nan's father said. "He'd divide his last crust with me. But I don't want to go where work is scarce. I must go where it is plentiful, where a man of even my age will be welcome."

"Your age, Papa Sherwood! How you talk," drawled Nan's mother in her pretty way. "You are as young as the best of 'em yet."

"Employers don't look at me through your pretty eyes, Momsey," he returned, laughing.

"Well," said his wife, still cheerfully, "my fishing seems to be resultless yet. Perhaps the bait's gone off the hook. Had I better haul in the line and bait again? I was always doing that when I went fishing with Adair and his brothers, years ago, when I was a little girl."

Her husband shook his head. "Have patience, Jessie," he said.

He had few expectations from the Memphis letter; yet there was a most surprising result from it on the way, something which by no possibility could the little family in the Amity Street cottage have suspected.

CHAPTER IV
SWEEPING CLEAN

"My goodness me!" ejaculated Bess Harley. "Talk about the 'leaden wings of Time.' Why! Time sweeps by us on electrically-driven, ball-bearing pinions. Here's another week gone, Nan, and tomorrow's Saturday."

"Yes," Nan agreed. "Time flies all too quickly, for me, anyway. The mills have been closed a week now."

"Oh, dear! That's all I hear," complained Bess. "Those tiresome old mills. Our Maggie's sister was crying in the kitchen last night because her Mike couldn't get a job now the mills were closed, and was drinking up all the money they had saved. That's what the mill-hands do; their money goes to the saloon-keepers!"

"The proportion of their income spent by the laboring class for alcoholic beverages is smaller by considerable than that spent by the well-to-do for similar poison!" quoted Nan decisively. "Mike is desperate, I suppose, poor fellow!"

"My goodness me!" cried Bess again. "You are most exasperating, Nan Sherwood. Mike's case has nothing to do with political Economy, and I do wish you'd drop that study out of school— —"

"I have!" gasped Nan, for just then her books slipped from her strap; "and history, rhetoric, and philosophical readings along with it," and she proceeded cheerfully to pick up the several books mentioned.

"You can't mean," Bess said, still severely, "that you won't go to Lakeview with me, Nan?"

"I wish you wouldn't keep saying that, Bess," Nan Sherwood cried. "Is it my fault? Don't you suppose I'd love to, if I could? We have no money. Father is out of work. There is no prospect of other work for him in Tillbury, he says, and," Nan continued desperately, "how do you suppose I can go to a fancy boarding school under these circumstances?"

"Why— —-"

For once Elizabeth was momentarily silenced. Suddenly her face brightened. "I tell you!" she exclaimed. "I'll speak to my father about it. He can fix it so that you will be able to go to the Hall with me, I know."

"I'd like to see myself an object of charity!" Nan cried, with heat. "I, guess, not! What I can't earn, or my father can't give me, I'll go without, Bess. That's all there is to that!"

Bess stared at her with quivering lips. "You can't be so mean, Nan," she faltered.

"I'm not mean!" denied the other.

"I'd like to know what you call it? Why, father'd never miss your tuition money in the world. And I know he'd pay your way if I asked him and told him how bad I felt about your not going."

"You're a dear, Bess!" declared Nan, impulsively hugging her friend again. "But you mustn't ask him, honey. It wouldn't be right, and I couldn't accept.

"Don't you understand, honey, that I have some pride in the matter? So have Papa Sherwood and Momsey. What they can't do for me their own selves I wouldn't want anybody to do."

"Why, that sounds awfully silly to me, Nan!" said Bess. "Why not take all you can get in this world? I'm sure I should."

"You don't know what you are saying," Nan returned seriously. "And, then, you are not poor, so you can afford to say it, and even do it."

"Poor! I'm getting to hate that word," cried Bess stormily. "It never bothered me before, much. We're not poor and none of our friends were poor. Not until those old mills closed. And now it seems all I hear is about folks being POOR. I hate it!"

"I guess," said Nan ruefully, "you don't hate it half as much as those of us who have to suffer it."

"I'm just going to find some way of getting you to Lakeview Hall, my dear," Bess rejoined gloomily. "Why! I won't want to go myself if you don't go, Nan."

Her friend thought she would better not tell Bess just then that the prospect was that she, with her father and mother, would have to leave Tillbury long before the autumn. Mr. Sherwood was trying to obtain a situation in Chicago, in a machine shop. He had no hope of getting another foreman's position.

Nothing had been heard from Mr. Adair MacKenzie, of Memphis. Mrs. Sherwood wanted to write again; but her husband begged her not to. He had a proper pride. It looked to him as though his wife's cousin did not care to be troubled by the necessities of his relations.

"We'll get along!" was Mr. Sherwood's repeated and cheerful statement. "Never say die! Hope is our anchor! Fate shall not balk us! And all the other copy-book maxims."

But it was Mrs. Sherwood and Nan who managed to save and scrimp and be frugal in many infinitesimal ways, thus making their savings last marvelously.

Nan gave up her entire Saturdays to household tasks. She insisted on that, and urged the curtailment of the weekly expense by having Mrs. Joyce come in to help but one day.

"I can iron, Momsey, and if I can't do it very well at first, I can learn," declared the plucky girl. "And, of course, I can sweep. That's good for me. Our physical instructor says so. Instead of going to the gym on Saturday, I'll put in calisthenics and acrobatic stunts with a broom and duster."

She was thorough, too. She could not have been her father's daughter without having that virtue. There was no "lick and a promise" in Nan Sherwood's housekeeping. She did not sweep the dust under the bureau, or behind the door, or forget to wipe the rounds of the chairs and the baseboard all around the rooms.

Papa Sherwood, coughing in the lower hall as the dust descended from above, declared she went through the cottage like a whirlwind. It was not as bad as that, but her vigorous young arms wielded the broom with considerable skill.

One Saturday, with every other room swept but the front hall, she closed the doors into that, and set wide open the outer door. There was more snow on the ground now; but the porch was cleaned and the path to the front gate neatly dug and swept. The tinkle of sleigh bells and the laughter of a crowd of her school friends swept by the corner of Amity Street. Nan ran out upon the porch and waved her duster at them.

There she stood, smiling out upon her little world for a minute. She might not see Amity Street, and the old neighbors, many weeks longer. A half-promise of work from the Chicago machine shop boss had reached Mr. Sherwood that morning by post. It seemed the only opening, and it meant that they would have to give up the "dwelling in amity" and go to crowded Chicago to live. For Momsey was determined that Papa Sherwood should not go without her.

Nan came back into the hall and began to wield the broom again. She could not leave the door open too long, for it was cold outside and the winter chill would get into the house. They had to keep all the rooms at an even temperature on account of Momsey's health.

But she swept vigorously, moving each piece of furniture, and throwing the rugs out upon the porch for a special sweeping there. The rough mat at the door was a heavy one. As Nan stooped to pick it up and toss it after the other small rugs, she saw the corner of a yellow envelope sticking from under the edge of the hall carpet.

"Wonder what that is?" murmured Nan. "Somebody has thrust a circular, or advertisement, under our door, and it's gone under the carpet. Yes! There's a tack out there."

She seized the corner of the envelope with thumb and finger. She drew it out. Its length surprised her. It was a long, official looking envelope, not bulky but most important looking. In the upper left-hand corner was printed:

ADAIR MACKENZIE & CO. STOCKS AND BONDS MEMPHIS

It was properly stamped and addressed to her mother. By the postmark on it Nan knew it must have been tucked under the door by the postman more than a week before. Somehow he had failed to ring their bell when he left the letter. The missing tack in the edge of the hall carpet had allowed the document to slide out of sight, and it might have been hidden for weeks longer had chance not shown the small corner of straw-colored paper to Nan.

She felt breathless. Her knees trembled. Somehow, Nan just KNEW that the letter from her mother's cousin must be of enormous importance. She set her broom in the corner and closed the door. It was fated that she should do no more sweeping that day.

CHAPTER V
GREAT EXPECTATIONS

Mr. Sherwood, in overalls and an old cap, had been sifting cinders out behind the shed. They had to be careful of fuel as well as of most other things. Momsey would not open the long envelope until he had been called and had come in. Nan still wore the bright colored bandana wound about her head, turban-wise, for a dust cap. Papa Sherwood beat the ashes from his hands as he stood before the glowing kitchen range.

"What is it?" he asked calmly. "A notice of a new tax assessment? Or a cure-all advertisement of Somebody's Pills?"

"It's from Cousin Adair," said Momsey, a little breathlessly. "And it's been lying at our door all the time."

"All what time?" asked Mr. Sherwood curiously.

"All the time we have been so disappointed in our inquiries elsewhere," said Momsey soberly.

"Oh!" responded her husband doubtfully, and said no more.

"It makes my knees shake," confessed Nan. "Do open it, Momsey!"

"I, I feel that it is important, too," the little lady said.

"Well, my dear," her husband finally advised, having waited in patience, "unless it is opened we shall never know whether your feeling is prophetic or not. 'By the itching of my thumb,' and so forth!"

Without making any rejoinder to this, and perhaps without hearing his gentle raillery, Mrs. Sherwood reached up to the coils of her thick hair to secure woman's never-failing implement, a hairpin.

There were two enclosures. Both she shook into her lap. The sealed, foreign-looking letter she picked up first. It was addressed in a clerkly hand to,

"MISTRESS JESSIE ADAIR BLAKE, "KINDNESS OF MESSRS. ADAIR MACKENZIE & CO. "MEMPHIS, TENN., U.S.A."

"From England. No! From Scotland," murmured Nan, looking over her mother's shoulder in her eagerness. She read the neatly printed card in the corner of the foreign envelope:

KELLAM & BLAKE HADBORNE CHAMBERS EDINBURGH

Mrs. Sherwood was whispering her maiden name over to herself. She looked up suddenly at her husband with roguish eyes.

"I'd almost forgotten there ever was such a girl as Jessie Adair Blake," she said.

"Oh, Momsey!" squealed Nan, with clasped hands and immense impatience. "Don't, DON'T be so slow! Open it!"

"No-o," her mother said, with pursed lips. "No, honey. The other comes first, I reckon."

It was a letter typewritten upon her cousin's letter-head; but it was not dictated by Mr. Adair MacKenzie. Instead, it was from Mr. MacKenzie's secretary, who stated that her employer had gone to Mexico on business that might detain him for several weeks.

"A letter addressed by you to Mr. MacKenzie arrived after his departure and is being held for him with other personal communications until his return; but being assured that you are the Jessie Adair Blake, now Sherwood—to whom the enclosed letter from Scotland is addressed, I take the liberty of forwarding the same. The Scotch letter reached us after Mr. MacKenzie's departure, likewise. Will you please acknowledge the receipt of the enclosure and oblige?"

This much of the contents of the secretary's letter was of particular interest to the Sherwoods. Momsey's voice shook a little as she finished reading it. Plainly she was disappointed.

"Cousin Adair, I am sure, would have suggested something helpful had he been at home," she said sadly. "It, it is a great disappointment, Robert."

"Well, well!" replied Mr. Sherwood, perhaps not without some secret relief. "It will all come out right. At least, your cousin hasn't refused his assistance. We shall be established somewhere before he returns from his Mexican trip."

"I, I did depend so much upon Adair's good will and advice," signed Momsey.

"But, dear me suz!" gasped Nan impatiently. "What are you folks bothering over that for? It isn't Cousin Adair that I want to know about. It's this letter, Momsey," and she seized the thin yet important envelope from Scotland and shook it before her mother's eyes.

"Better look into it, Momsey," advised Mr. Sherwood easily, preparing to return to the cinder sifting. "Maybe it's from some of your relatives in the Old Country. I see 'Blake' printed in the corner. Didn't your father have an uncle or somebody, who was steward on the estate of a Scotch Laird of some renown?"

"Heck, mon!" cried Momsey, with her usual gaiety, and throwing off the cloud of gloom that had momentarily subdued her spirit. "Ye air a wise cheil. Ma faither talked muckle o' Uncle Hughie Blake, remimberin' him fra' a wee laddie when his ain faither took him tae Scotland, and tae Castle Emberon, on a veesit."

Nan and Papa Sherwood laughed at her when she assumed the Scotch burr of her forebears. With precision she cut the flap of this smaller envelope. She felt no excitement now. She had regained control of herself after the keen disappointment arising from the first letter.

She calmly opened the crackly sheet of legal looking paper in her lap. It was not a long letter, and it was written in a stiff, legal hand, instead of being typewritten, each character as precise as the legal mind that dictated it:

"Mistress Jessie Adair Blake, (Known to be a married woman, but wedded name unknown to writer.)

"Dear Madam: It is my duty to inform you that your father (the late Randolph Hugh Blake) was made sole beneficiary of his late uncle, Mr. Hugh Blake, the Laird of Emberon's steward, by a certain testament, or will, made many years ago. Mr. Hugh Blake has recently died a bachelor, and before his demise he added a codicil to the above testament, or will, naming you, his great niece, his sole heir and beneficiary.

"There are other relatives who may make some attempt to oppose your claim; but none of near blood. Your title to the said estate is clear; but it is quite necessary that you should appear before our Courts with proofs of identity, and so forth. On receipt from you of acknowledgment of this letter, with copies of identification papers (your grandfather's naturalization papers, your father's discharge from army, your own birth certificate and marriage lines, and so forth) I will give myself the pleasure of forwarding any further particulars you may wish, and likewise place at your command my own services in obtaining possession for you of your great uncle's estate.

"The said estate of Mr. Hugh Blake, deceased, amounts, in real and personal property, including moneys in the bank, to about the sum, roughly estimated, of 10,000 pounds.

"Respectfully, your servant,

"Andrew Blake, Solicitor and Att'y."

Nan had leaned over her mother's shoulder, big-eyed, scarce believing the plainly written words she read. It was preposterous, ridiculous, fanciful, a dream from which she must awake in a moment to the full realization of their dreadful need of just such a godsend as this.

It was her father's voice that roused the girl. He had not seen the letter and Momsey had read it silently to herself.

"Look out, Nancy! What is the matter with your mother?"

With a cry the girl caught the frail little lady in her arms as the letter slipped unheeded from her lap to the floor. Mrs. Sherwood's eyes were closed. She had fainted.

CHAPTER VI
A SPRAT FOR A HERRING

"I don't need the doctor this time, honey; joy never killed yet"

So said Mrs. Sherwood, opening her eyes to see the scared face of Nan close above her. Then she saw her husband at her feet, quietly chafing her hands in his own hard, warm palms. She pulled hers gently from his clasp and rested them upon his head. Mr. Sherwood's hair was iron-gray, thick, and inclined to curl. She ran her little fingers into it and clung tightly.

"Let, let me get my breath!" she gasped. Then, after a moment she smiled brilliantly into the wind-bitten face of the kneeling man. "It's all over, Robert," she said.

"My dear!" he cried thickly; while Nan could not wholly stifle the cry of fear that rose to her lips.

"It's all over," repeated the little woman. "All the worry, all the poverty, all the uncertainty, all the hard times."

Mr. Sherwood looked startled indeed. He had no idea what the letter from Scotland contained, and he feared that his wife, who had already suffered so much, was for the moment quite out of her head.

"My poor Jessie," he began, but her low, sweet laugh stopped him.

"Not poor! Never poor again, Robert!" she cried. "God is very good to us. At the very darkest hour He has shown us the dawn. Robert, we are rich!"

"Great goodness, Jessie! What do you mean? Exclaimed Mr. Sherwood, stumbling to his feet at last.

"It's true! It's true, Papa Sherwood!" Nan cried, clapping her hands. "Don't you call ten thousand dollars riches?"

"Ten, thousand, dollars?" murmured her father. He put his hand to his head and looked confusedly about for a seat, into which he weakly dropped. Nan had picked up the letter and now she dramatically thrust it into his hand.

"Read that, Papa Sherwood!" she said commandingly.

He read the communication from the Scotch attorney, first with immense surprise, then with profound doubt. Who but a young imaginative girl, like Nan, or a woman with unbounded faith in the miracles of God, like her mother, could accept such a perfectly wonderful thing as being real?

"A hoax," thought the man who had worked so hard all his life without the least expectation of ever seeing a penny that he did not earn himself. "Can it be that any of those heedless relatives of my wife's in Memphis have attempted a practical joke at this time?"

He motioned for Nan to bring him the envelope, too. This he examined closely, and then read the communication again. It looked all regular. The stationery, the postmark, the date upon it, all seemed perfectly in accord.

Mrs. Sherwood's gay little laugh shattered the train of her husband's thought. "I know what the matter is with you, Papa Sherwood," she said. "You think it must be a practical joke."

"Oh!" gasped Nan, feeling a positive pain at her heart. This awful possibility had never entered her mind before.

"But it isn't," went on her mother blithely. "It is real. Mr. Hugh Blake, of Emberon, must have been very old; and he was probably as saving and canny as any Scotchman who ever wore kilts. It is not surprising that he should have left an estate of considerable size— —-"

"Ten thousand dollars!" breathed Nan again. She loved to repeat it. There was white magic in the very sound of such a sum of money. But her father threw a conversational bomb into their midst the next instant.

"Ten thousand dollars, you goosey!" he said vigorously. "That's the main doubt in the whole business. It isn't ten thousand dollars. It's fifty thousand dollars! A pound, either English or Scotch, is almost five of our dollars. Ten thousand dollars would certainly be a fortune for us; fifty thousand is beyond the dreams of avarice."

"Oh, dear me!" said Nan weakly.

But Mrs. Sherwood merely laughed again. "The more the better," she said. "Why shouldn't we be able to put fifty thousand dollars to good use?"

"Oh, we can, Momsey," said Nan eagerly. "But, will we be let?"

Mr. Sherwood laughed grimly at that; but his wife continued confidently:

"I am sure nobody needs it more than we do."

"Why!" her daughter said, just as excitedly, "we'll be as rich as Bess Harley's folks. Oh, Momsey! Oh, Papa Sherwood! Can I go to Lakewood Hall?"

The earnestness of her cry showed the depths to which that desire had plumbed during these last weeks of privation and uncertainty. It was Nan's first practical thought in relation to the possibility of their changed circumstances.

The father and mother looked at each other with shocked understanding. The surprise attending the letter had caused both parents to forget, for the moment, the effect of this wonderful promise of fortune, whether true or false, on imaginative, high-spirited Nan.

"Let us be happy at first, Nan, just in the knowledge that some money is coming to us," Mrs. Sherwood said more quietly. "Never mind how much, or how little. Time will tell all that."

"Now you talk like father," cried Nan, pouting.

"And let father talk a little, too," Mr. Sherwood said, smiling, "and to you both." His right forefinger struck the letter emphatically in his other hand. "This is a very wonderful, a blessed, thing, if true. But it has to be proven. We must build our hopes on no false foundation."

"Oh, Papa Sherwood! How can we, when the man says there— —-"

"Hush!" whispered Momsey, squeezing her excited little daughter's hand.

"In the first place," continued Mr. Sherwood quietly and gravely, "there may be some mistake in the identification of your mother, child, as the niece mentioned in this old man's will."

"Oh!" Nan could not help that gasp.

"Again, there may be stronger opposition to her claim than this lawyer at present sees. Fifty thousand dollars is a whole lot of money, and other people by the name of Blake will be tempted by it."

"How mean of them!" whispered Nan.

"And, above all," pursued Mr. Sherwood, "this may be merely a scheme by unprincipled people to filch small sums of money from gullible people. The 'foreign legacy swindle' is worked in many different ways. There may be calls for money, by this man who names himself Andrew Blake, for preliminary work on the case. We haven't much; but if he is baiting for hundreds of Blakes in America he may secure, in the aggregate, a very tidy sum indeed."

"Oh, Father!" cried Nan. "That's perfectly horrid!"

"But perfectly possible. Let us not swallow this bait, hook, line and sinker. You see, he sends no copy of the will in question, or that codicil relating to your mother's legacy; nor does he offer identification or surety as to his own standing. Don't let the possibilities of this wonderful thing carry you off your feet, my dear."

Nan's lip was quivering and she could scarcely crowd back the tears. To have one's hopes rise so high only to be dashed— —-.

"Don't completely crush us, Papa Sherwood, with your perfectly unanswerable logic," said his wife lightly. "We'll remember all these strictures, and more. We can at least put the matter to the test."

"Quite so," agreed her husband. "We will prepare the papers requested by this Scotch attorney. I will even inquire of a good lawyer here something regarding the Scotch laws in such a matter as this, if it will be necessary to make a personal appearance before the local courts over there. And perhaps we can find out the true standing of Mr. Andrew Blake, of Kellam & Blake, Edinburgh. It will cost us a little money, and we can ill spare it now; but to satisfy ourselves— —-"

"We will throw a sprat to catch a herring," quoted Momsey cheerfully.

"Quite so," repeated Mr. Sherwood.

"But, dear, DEAR!" moaned Nan. "Is that all it is going to amount to? Don't you really believe it's all true, Papa Sherwood?"

"I can't say that I do, my dear," returned her father gravely. "Such romantic things as this do not often happen outside of story books."

"Then, I declare!" cried Nan desperately, "I wish we lived in a story book!"

"Your father will make inquiries at once, honey," said Momsey easily, seemingly very little disturbed herself by her husband's doubts and fears. To her mind this wonderful turn of fortune's wheel was in direct answer to prayer. Nothing could shake her faith in the final result of her husband's inquiries. Yet, she was proud of his caution and good sense.

"I do think it is dreadful," murmured Nan, "to believe one's self rich for only a minute!"

"Have patience, honey," said her mother.

"Meanwhile," added Mr. Sherwood, rising, "I will go back to sifting cinders."

But Nan did no more sweeping that day.

CHAPTER VII
A VISTA OF NEW FORTUNES

Nan said nothing to Bess Harley, her particular chum and confidant, about the wonderful letter that had come from Scotland. Although Momsey and Nan talked the legacy over intimately that Saturday afternoon, and planned what they would really do with some of the money "when their ship came in," the young girl knew that the matter was not to be discussed outside of the family circle.

Not even the hope Nan now cherished of accompanying her chum to Lakeview Hall when the next school year opened was divulged when the two girls were together on Sunday, or on the days that immediately followed.

Nan Sherwood went about her household and school tasks in a sort of waking dream. Imagination was continually weaving pictures in her mind of what might happen if the vista of new fortunes that had opened before the little family in the Amity Street cottage really came true.

Papa Sherwood's first reports on the matter of the Scotch legacy were not inspiring.

"Mr. Bludsoe says we'd better go slow," he said seriously. Mr. Bludsoe was a lawyer of high repute in Tillbury. "This letter may be written by an attorney in Edinburgh; but there are rascally lawyers there as well as elsewhere. Bludsoe had correspondents in London. They may be able to inform him regarding the firm of solicitors, Kellam & Blake, if the firm really is entered at the Scotch bar."

"Oh! But won't that mean delay?" murmured Nan.

"Meanwhile," said her father, smiling at her impatience, "we will prepare the papers identifying your dear mother so that, if this wonderful new fortune should be a reality, we can put in a proper claim for it. Just the same," he added to his wife, when Nan had left the room, "I have written to that machine shop boss in Chicago that I am ready to come to work any day he may send for me."

"Oh, Robert!" gasped the little lady. "Won't you believe?"

"Like the darkey who was asked if he believed the world was round, and said, 'Ah believes it, but Ah ain't dead sho' of it.' I presume this great fortune is possible, Jessie, but I haven't perfect and abiding faith in its existence, FOR us," said her husband.

But Momsey had just that quality of faith. She went singing about her household tasks and her usual smile beamed quite beatific. So said Dr. Christian, who stepped in to see her, as was his custom every few days.

"What's this? What's this?" the old medical practitioner demanded of Mr. Sherwood, on the porch, where he usually made his report, and to which Nan often stole to listen openly to them discuss her mother's case. "I find her in a state of happy excitement, and that is quite right, Robert, quite right, if the hopes that are the wellspring of it are not quenched. What does it mean? Have you arranged the sea voyage I advised?"

Papa Sherwood's face changed suddenly. He looked oddly, Nan thought, at the doctor. "I don't know but that is it, Doc," he said. "That sea voyage may be in the offing."

"Best thing that could happen to her, best thing that could happen to her!" declared the old physician with emphasis, as he stumped away.

Nan wondered what that could mean. A sea voyage for Momsey? Of course, for all of them. She could not imagine Momsey going anywhere without her and Papa Sherwood.

She knew she was not to say anything about what she heard pass between her father and the doctor on the porch. Indeed, Nan was no bearer of tales in any event. But she was very curious. The steam from the cauldron of Mystery seldom arose in the little "dwelling in amity" save about Christmas time or just previous to Nan's birthday. But Papa Sherwood certainly was enigmatical and Momsey was mysteriously happy, as Dr. Christian had said.

"And we'll put steam heat in the little house. You know, Robert, we've always wanted to," Nan's mother suddenly said one evening as they all sat around the reading lamp, and quite apropos of nothing at all. Then she laughed, flushing prettily. "There! You see what my mind runs on. I really can't help it."

It was only a day or two later that the second letter came from Memphis. Mr. Adair MacKenzie had returned from Mexico and evidently one of the first duties he performed was to write his Cousin Jessie his congratulations.

"A letter on quite another matter," this epistle read, "from our distant kinsman, Andrew Blake, of Kellam & Blake, apprised me that the ancient Hugh Blake, steward to the Lairds of Emberon for so many years, was dead and that his property was willed to your father, whose appearance as a lad at Emberon pleased the old man greatly.

"You are to be congratulated. The estate is considerable, I understand. Your husband's troubles which are mentioned in your letter that I found awaiting my return will now be over. For, although Andrew Blake intimates that there may be considerable opposition in the courts there, over the money going to an American heir, you will be able in the end to establish your rights.

"Believe me, my dear Jessie, I know of nobody in our family to whom I would rather see fortune come than to yourself and your dear ones. If I can be of any assistance, financially, or otherwise, in helping you obtain your rights in this event, believe me, I stand ready to give such aid. Do not hesitate to call upon me. My regards to your husband and little girl whom I have never seen; Alice and John join me in expressing our good wishes for your happy future. I remain, with the old love I always had for you, Your cousin, Adair MacKenzie."

"Now, Robert, what have you to say?" cried Momsey triumphantly, while Nan danced a fandango about the room.

"This much," replied her husband, smiling. "Our minds are relieved on one point, at least. Kellam & Blake are respectable attorneys. We will send our communication to Mr. Blake at once, without waiting for Mr. Bludsoe's enquiries to bear fruit. Your Cousin Adair knows the Scotch firm, and of course vouches for their trustworthiness."

"Dear me, Papa Sherwood, you are so practical!" sighed Nan. She meant "vexing;" they were interchangeable terms to her mind at this exciting point. "Can't you work up any enthusiasm over Momsey's wonderful fortune?"

"Its existence is established, it would seem, beyond peradventure," said Mr. Sherwood drily. "But our attempt to obtain the fortune is not yet begun."

"Why, ee!" squealed Nan. "You don't really suppose anybody will try to keep Momsey from getting it?"

"Exactly that," said her father. "The Blakes are a widely scattered clan. There are probably a number of people as close in blood-tie to the old man who has just died as your mother, my dear. These people may all bob up, one after another, to dispute Momsey's claim."

"But, dear me!" gasped Nan. "The money was willed to Momsey."

"Nevertheless, these other relatives, if there be such—can keep Momsey out of the enjoyment of her rights for a long time. Court processes are slow, and especially so, I should judge, among the canny and careful Scotch. I think we would better leave it to the lawyers to settle. We cannot hasten the courts by worrying over the fortune.

"I think," pursued Papa Sherwood judiciously, "that instead of spending our time discussing and dreaming of the fortune in Scotland, we would better go right on with our tasks here as though there were really no fortune at all."

"Oh, my!" whispered Nan, her eyes clouding. "That's because of my last fortnightly report. I know I fell behind in history and rhetoric."

"Don't be too hard on us, Papa Sherwood," said Momsey brightly. "Anticipation is more than half of every pleasure. I lie awake every night and spend this great fortune of ours to the very last penny."

"Of course," the little lady added, with more gravity, "I wouldn't really spend fifty thousand dollars so recklessly as I do in my mind. But I can found schools, and hospitals, and educate Nan, and give you, Papa Sherwood, a great big business, and buy two automobiles, and— —-"

"Enough! Enough!" cried Mr. Sherwood, in mock seriousness. "You are a born spendthrift, Momsey. That you have had no chance to really be one thus far will only make your case more serious when you have this legacy in your possession. Two automobiles, no less!"

"But I want you both, my dears, to bear one very important fact in mind. Roughly estimated the fortune is ten thousand pounds. To be exact, it may be a good deal less at the start. Then, after the lawyers and the courts get through with the will and all, the remainder that dribbles into your pocket, Momsey, may be a very small part of ten thousand pounds."

"Oh, how horrid, Papa Sherwood!" cried Nan. "We won't listen to him, will we, Momsey?"

"Oh, yes we will," her mother said quietly, but smiling. "But we will still believe that the world is good and that God has given us great good fortune. Papa talks very sensibly; but I know that there is nothing to fear. We are going to be very well off for the rest of our lives, and I cannot be thankful enough for it."

At that Mr. Sherwood literally threw up his hands. "Nevertheless," he said, "I expect to go to Chicago next Monday, to begin work in the machine shop. The boss writes me that I can come at that time."

"I will get your clothes ready for you, Robert," said Momsey calmly. "Perhaps you will feel better in your mind if you keep busy during this time of waiting."

CHAPTER VIII
TWO IMPORTANT HAPPENINGS

It happened, however, that Mr. Sherwood did not go to Chicago to work in the machine shop. Something happened before the week was out, that quite put his intention aside.

Indeed, Nan declared that two important happenings just then changed the current of affairs at the little cottage on Amity Street and that she had a principal part in the action of the first of these unexpected happenings.

It was lovely skating on Norway Pond, and both Nan and her chum, Bess Harley, were devoted to the sport. Nan had been unable to be on the ice Saturdays, because of her home tasks; but when her lessons were learned, she was allowed to go after supper.

It happened to be just at the dark of the moon this week; that kept many off the ice, although the weather was settled and the ice was perfectly safe. Sometimes the boys built a bonfire on Woody Point, with refuse from the planing mill, and that lit up a good bit of the ice.

But once out on the pond, away from the shadows cast by the high banks, the girls could see well enough. They were both good skaters, and with arms crossed and hands clasped, they swung up the middle of the pond in fine style.

"I just love to skate with you, Nan," sighed Bess ecstatically. "You move just like my other self. We're Siamese twins. We strike out together perfectly. Oh, my dear! I don't see whatever I am to do if you refuse to go to Lakeview with me."

Nan could scarcely keep from telling Bess of the wonderful new fortune that seemed about to come to her; but she was faithful to her home training, and only said:

"Don't fret about it, honey. Maybe something will turn up to let me go."

"If you'd let my father pay your way——-?" insinuated Bess.

"Don't talk of that. It's impossible," said Nan decisively. "It's a long time yet to fall. Maybe conditions will be different at home. A dozen things may happen before school opens in September."

"Yes! But they may not be the right things," sighed Bess.

She could not be too melancholy on such a night as this, however. It was perfectly quiet, and the arch of the sky was like black velvet pricked out with gold and silver stars. Their soft radiance shed some light upon the pond, enough, at least, to show the girl chums the way before them as they skimmed on toward Powerton Landing.

They had left a noisy crowd of boys behind them, near the stamp Factory, mostly mill boys, and the like. Bess had been taught at home to shrink from association with the mill people and that is why she had urged Nan to take this long skate up the pond. Around the Tillbury end of it they were always falling in with little groups of mill boys and girls whom Bess did not care to meet.

There was another reason this evening for keeping away from the stamp factory, too. The manager of that big shop had hired a gang of ice cutters a few days before, and had filled his own private icehouse. The men had cut out a roughly outlined square of the thick ice, sawed it into cakes, and poled it to shore and so to the sleds and the manager's icehouse.

It was not a large opening in the ice; but even if the frost continued, it would be several days before the new ice would form thickly enough to bear again over that spot.

Elsewhere, however, the ice was strong, for all the cutting for the big icehouses had been done long before near the Landing. The lights of Powerton Landing were twinkling ahead of them as the two friends swept on up the long lake. The wind was in their faces, such wind as there was, and the air was keen and nippy.

The action of skating, however, kept Nan and Bess warm. Bess in her furs and Nan in her warm tam-o'-shanter and the muffler Momsey had knitted with her own hands, did not mind the cold.

The evening train shrieked out of the gap and across the long trestle just beyond the landing, where it halted for a few seconds for passengers to embark or to leave the cars. This train was from Chicago, and on Monday Papa Sherwood expected to go to that big city to work.

The thought gave Nan a feeling of depression. The little family in the Amity street cottage had never been separated for more than a day since she could remember. It was going to be hard on Momsey, with Papa Sherwood away and Nan in school all day. How were they going to get along without Papa Sherwood coming home to supper, and doing the hard chores?

Bess awoke her chum from these dreams. "Dear me, Nan! Have you lost your tongue all of a sudden? Do say something, or do something."

"Let's race the train down the pond to Tillbury," proposed Nan instantly.

The lights of the long coaches were just moving out of the station at the Landing. The two girls came about in a graceful curve and struck out for home at a pace that even the train could not equal. The rails followed the shore of the pond on the narrow strip of lowland at the foot of the bluffs. They could see the lights shining through the car windows all the way.

The fireman threw open the door of his firebox to feed the furnace and a great glare of light, and a shower of sparks, spouted from the smokestack. The rumble of the wheels from across the ice seemed louder than usual.

"Come on, Bess!" gasped Nan, quite excited. "We can do better than this! Why, that old train will beat us!"

For they were falling behind. The train hooted its defiance as it swept down toward Woody Point. The girls shot in toward the shore, where the shadow of the high bluff lay heavily upon the ice.

They heard the boys' voices somewhere below them, but Bess and Nan could not see them yet. They knew that the boys had divided into sides and were playing old-fashioned hockey, "shinny-on-your-own-side" as it was locally called. Above the rumbling of the train they heard the crack of the shinny-stick against the wooden block, and the "z-z-z-zip!" of the missile as it scaled over the ice.

"Those boys will get into the ice-hole if they don't look out," Nan had just said to her chum, when suddenly a wild yell arose from the hockey players.

The train was slowing down at the signal tower, and finally stopped there. A freight had got in on the main track which had to be cleared before the passenger train could go into Tillbury station. The coaches stood right along the edge of the frozen pond.

But it was nothing in connection with the evening train that caused such a commotion among the skaters near the stamp factory. There was a crash of breaking ice and a scrambling of skaters away from the spot. The boys' yells communicated panic to other people ashore.

"He's in! He's in!" Nan and Bess heard the boys yelling. Then a man's voice took up the cry: "He'll be drowned! Help! Help!"

"That's old Peter Newkirk," gasped Nan, squeezing Bess' gloved hands tightly. "He's night watchman at the stamp works, and he has only one arm. He can't help that boy."

The youngsters who had been playing hockey so recklessly near the thin ice, were not as old as Nan and Bess, and the accident had thrown them into utter confusion. Some skated for the shore, screaming for ropes and fence-rails; others only tried to get away from the danger spot themselves. None did the first thing to help their comrade who had broken through the ice.

"Where are you going, Nan?" gasped Bess, pulling back. "You'll have us both in the water, too."

"We can save him! Quick!" returned her chum eagerly.

She let go of Bess and unwound the long muffler from about her own neck. "If we could only see him!" the girl said, over and over.

And then a brilliant idea struck Nan Sherwood, and she turned to shout to old Peter Newkirk on the shore. "Peter! Peter! Turn on the electric light sign! Turn it on so we can see where he's gone in!"

The watchman had all his wits about him. There was a huge electric sign on the stamp works roof, advertising the company's output. The glare of it could be seen for miles, and it lit up brilliantly the surroundings of the mill.

Peter Newkirk bounded away to the main door of the works. The switch that controlled the huge sign was just inside that door. Before Nan and Bess had reached the edge of the broken ice, the electricity was suddenly shot into the sign and the whole neighborhood was alight.

"I see him! There he is!" gasped Nan to her chum. "Hold me tight by the skirt, Bess! We'll get him!"

She flung herself to her knees and stopped sliding just at the edge of the old, thick ice. With a sweep of her strong young arm she shot the end of the long muffler right into the clutching hands of the drowning boy.

Involuntarily he seized it. He had been down once, and submersion in the ice water had nearly deprived him of both consciousness and power to help save himself. But Nan drew him quickly through the shattered ice-cakes to the edge of the firm crystal where she knelt.

"We have him! We have him!" she cried, in triumph. "Give me your hand, boy! I won't let you go down again."

But to lift him entirely out of the water would have been too much for her strength. However, several men came running now from the stalled passenger train. The lighting of the electric sign had revealed to them what was going on upon the pond.

The man who lifted the half-drowned boy out of the water was not one of the train crew, but a passenger. He was a huge man in a bearskin coat and felt boots. He was wrapped up so heavily, and his fur cap was pulled down so far over his ears and face, that Nan could not see what he really looked like. In a great, gruff voice he said:

"Well, now! Give me a girl like you ev'ry time! I never saw the beat of it. Here, mister!" as he put the rescued boy into the arms of a man who had just run from a nearby house. "Get him between blankets and he'll be all right. But he's got this smart little girl to thank that he's alive at all."

He swung around to look at Nan again. Bess was crying frankly, with her gloved hands before her face. "Oh, Nan! Nan!" she sobbed. "I didn't do a thing, not a thing. I didn't even hang to the tail of your skirt as you told me. I, I'm an awful coward."

The big man patted Nan's shoulder lightly. "There's a little girl that I'm going to see here in Tillbury," he said gruffly. "I hope she turns out to be half as smart as you are, sissy." Then he tramped back to the train that was just then starting.

Nan began to laugh. "Did you hear that funny man?" she asked Bess. "Do stop your crying, Bess! You have no reason to cry. You are not hurt."

"But, but you might have been, been drowned, too," sobbed her chum. "I didn't help you a mite."

"Bother!" exclaimed Nan Sherwood. "Don't let's talk about it. We'll go home. I guess we've both had enough skating for tonight."

Bess wiped away her tears and clung to Nan's hand all the way to their usual corner for separating. Nan ran home from there quickly and burst into the kitchen to find Momsey and Papa Sherwood in the midst of a very serious conference.

"What is the matter?" cried Nan, startled by the gravity of her father and the exaltation upon her mother's face. "What's happened?"

"A very great thing, Nan, honey," said Momsey, drawing her daughter to her side. "Tell her, Papa Sherwood."

He sighed deeply and put away the letter they had been reading. "It's from Mr. Blake, of Edinburgh," he said. "I can no longer doubt the existence of the fortune, my dears. But I fear we shall have to strive for it in the Scotch courts."

"Oh!" cried Nan, under her breath.

"Mr. Blake tells us here that it is absolutely necessary for us to come to Scotland, and for your mother to appear in person before the court there. The sum of money and other property willed to Momsey by her great uncle is so large that the greatest care will be exercised by the Scotch judges to see that it goes to the right person."

"As your mother once said, we must throw a sprat to catch a herring. In this case we shall be throwing a sprat to catch a whale! For the amount of money we may have to spend to secure the fifty thousand dollars left by Mr. Hugh Blake, of Emberon, is small, in comparison to the fortune itself.

"We must go to Scotland," finished Mr. Sherwood firmly. "And we must start as soon as possible."

CHAPTER IX
ON THE WAY TO THE WILDERNESS

It seemed to Nan Sherwood that night as though she never could get to sleep. Her mind and imagination worked furiously.

Momsey and Papa Sherwood had sent her to bed early. There had been no time to tell them about the accident on the ice and her part in it. Her parents had much to discuss, much to decide upon. The Scotch lawyer urged their presence before the court having jurisdiction in the matter of the late Mr. Hugh Blake's will, and that as soon as they could cross the ocean.

Transportation from the little Illinois town, across the intervening states to the seaport, and thence, over the winter ocean to Glasgow, and so on by rail to Edinburgh, was a journey the contemplation of which, to such a quiet family as the Sherwoods, was nothing less than appalling.

And there were many things to take into consideration that Nan did not wholly understand. Mrs. Sherwood would require her husband's undivided attention while she made the long and arduous journey. The sea voyage was right in line with the physician's opinion of what was needed to restore her health; but it was a venture at best.

Had the family possessed plenty of money it is doubtful if Mr. Sherwood would have risked more than a coasting voyage. Conditions rising out of the legacy from the great uncle in Scotland spelled necessity in this case. Of the little sum left in bank, most of it would be required to pay the fares of Mr. and Mrs. Sherwood to Edinburgh, and their modest living there for a few weeks. There was not enough money in hand to pay a third passage and the expenses of a third person in Scotland, until the court business should be settled.

Mr. Sherwood had already taken Mr. Bludsoe, the lawyer, into his confidence. He could make arrangements through him to mortgage the cottage if it became absolutely necessary. He shrank from accepting financial help from Mrs. Sherwood's relatives in Memphis.

Besides, decision must be made immediately. Plans must be made almost overnight. They must start within forty-eight hours to catch a certain steamer bound for the Scotch port of Glasgow, as Mr. Sherwood had already found out. And all their questions resolved finally into this very important one:

"WHAT SHALL WE DO ABOUT NAN?"

Nan, in her little white bed, had no idea that she was the greatest difficulty her parents found in this present event. It never entered her busy mind that Papa Sherwood and Momsey would dream of going to Scotland without her.

"What shall we do with Nan?" Momsey said over and over again. She realized as well as did Mr. Sherwood that to take the child was an utter impossibility. Their financial circumstances, as well as other considerations would not allow it.

Yet, what should they do with her, with whom to trust her during their uncertain absence on the other side? No answer that came to their minds seemed the right one. They rose that wintry morning without having this most important of all questions decided.

This was Sunday and Mrs. Joyce always came over for breakfast; for she lived alone and never had any too much to eat, Nan was sure. As for the old woman's eating with the family, that was a fiction she kept up for appearance's sake, perhaps, or to salve her own claims to former gentility. She always set a place for herself at the family table in the dining room and then was too busy to eat with them, taking her own meal in the kitchen.

Therefore it was she only who heard the commanding rap at the kitchen door in the midst of the leisurely meal, and answered it.

Just then Nan had dropped her knife and fork and was staring from Momsey's pitying face to Papa Sherwood's grave one, as she cried, in a whisper:

"Not me? Oh, my dears! You're never going without me, all that long journey? What, whatever shall I do without you both?"

"Don't, honey! Don't say it that way!" begged Momsey, putting her handkerchief to her eyes.

"If it was not quite impossible, do you think for a moment, daughter, that we would contemplate leaving you at home?" queried Mr. Sherwood, his own voice trembling.

"It, it seems impossible!" gasped Nan, "just as though it couldn't be. I won't know what to do without you, my dears. And what will you do without me?"

That seemed to be unanswerable, and it quite broke Momsey down. She sobbed openly into her handkerchief.

"Who's going to be her little maid?" demanded Nan, of her father. "Who's going to 'do' her beautiful hair? Who's going to wait on her when she has her dreadful headaches? And who's going to play 'massagist' like me? I want to know who can do all those things for Momsey if you take her away from me, Papa Sherwood?" and she ended quite stormily.

"My dear child!" Mr. Sherwood said urgently. "I want you to listen to me. Our situation is such that we cannot possibly take you with us. That is final. It is useless for us to discuss the point, for there is nothing to be gained by discussing it from now till Doomsday."

Nan gulped down a sob and looked at him with dry eyes. Papa Sherwood had never seemed so stern before, and yet his own eyes were moist. She began to see that this decision was very hard upon her parents, too.

"Now do you understand," he asked gently, "that we cannot take our little daughter with us, but that we are much worried by the fact, and we do not know what to do with her while we are gone?"

"You, you might as well put me in an orphan asylum," choked Nan. "I'll be an orphan till you get back."

"Oh, honey!" cried her mother.

"There now!" said Nan, jumping up quickly and going around the table to her mother's side. "You poor dear! I won't say anything more to hurt and trouble you. I'm a selfish thing, that's what I am."

Momsey wound her arms about her. Papa Sherwood still looked grave. "We get no nearer to the proper solution of the difficulty," he said. "Of course, Nancy, the orphan asylum is out of the question."

"I'll stay here, of course," Nan said, with some difficulty keeping her voice from quavering.

"Not alone in the house, honey," Momsey said quickly.

"With Mrs. Joyce?" suggested Nan tentatively.

"No," Mr. Sherwood said. "She is not the person to be trusted with you."

"There's Mrs. Grimes' boarding house around the corner?" suggested Nan.

Momsey shuddered. "Never! Never! My little girl in a boarding house. Oh, Papa Sherwood! We must find somebody to care for her while we are away, who loves Nan."

And it was just here that a surprisingly gruff voice took up the matter and decided it in a moment.

"That's me," said the voice, with conviction. "She's just the sort of little girl I cotton to, sister Jessie. And Kate'll be fairly crazy about her. If you're going anywhere for a long spell, just let me take her up to Pine Camp. We have no little girls up there, never had any. But I bet we know how to treat 'em."

"Hen!" shouted Mr. Sherwood, stumbling up from the table, and putting out both hands to the big man whom Mrs. Joyce had ushered in from the kitchen so unexpectedly.

"Henry Sherwood!" gasped Momsey, half rising herself in her surprise and delight.

"Why!" cried Nan, "it's the bear-man!" for Mr. Henry Sherwood wore the great fur coat and cap that he had worn the evening before when he had come to Nan's aid in rescuing the boy from Norway Pond.

Afterward Nan confessed, naively, that she ought to have known he was her Uncle Henry. Nobody, she was quite sure, could be so big and brawny as the lumberman from Michigan.

"She's the girl for me," proclaimed Uncle Henry admiringly. "Smart as a whip and as bold as a catamount. Hasn't she told you what she did last night? Sho! Of course not. She don't go 'round blowing about her deeds of valor, I bet!" and the big man went off into a gale of laughter that seemed to shake the little cottage.

Papa Sherwood and Momsey had to learn all the particulars then, and both glowed with pride over their little daughter's action. Gradually, after numerous personal questions were asked and answered on both sides, the conversation came around to the difficulty the little family was in, and the cause of it.

Henry Sherwood listened to the story of the Scotch legacy with wide-open eyes, marveling greatly. The possibility of his brother's wife becoming wealthy amazed and delighted his simple mind. The fact that they had to take the long journey to Scotland to obtain the money troubled him but little. Although he had never traveled far himself, save to Chicago from the Michigan woods, Mr. Henry Sherwood had lived in the open so much that distances did not appall him.

"Sure you'll go," he proclaimed, reaching down into a very deep pocket and dragging to light a long leather pouch, with a draw-string of home-cured deer skin. "And if you are short, Bob, we'll go down into this poke and see what there is left.

"I came down to Chicago to see about a piece of timber that's owned by some sharps on Jackson Street. I didn't know but I might get to cut that timber. I've run it careless-like, and I know pretty near what there is in it. So I said to Kate:

"'I'll see Bob and his wife, and the little nipper— —-"

"Goodness!" ejaculated Nan, under her breath.

Uncle Henry's eyes twinkled and the many wrinkles about them screwed up into hard knots. "Beg pardon!" he exclaimed, for his ears were very sharp. "This young lady, I should have said. Anyhow, I told Kate I'd see you all and find out what you were doing.

"Depending on mills and such for employment isn't any very safe way to live, I think. Out in the woods you are as free as air, and there aren't so many bosses, and you don't have to think much about 'the market' and 'supply and demand,' and all that."

"Just the same," said Mr. Robert Sherwood, his own eyes twinkling, "you are in some trouble right now, I believe, Hen?"

"Sho! You've got me there," boomed his brother with a great laugh. "But there aren't many reptiles like old Ged Raffer. And we can thank a merciful Creator for that. I expect there are just a few miserly old hunks like Ged as horrible examples to the rest of us."

"What is the nature of your trouble with this old fellow?" asked Mr. Robert Sherwood.

"We've got hold on adjoining options. I had my lines run by one of the best surveyors in the Peninsula of Michigan. But he up and died. Ged claims I ran over on his tract about a mile. He got to court first, got an injunction, and tied me all up in a hard legal knot until the state surveyors can go over both pieces of timber. The land knows when that'll be! Those state surveyors take a week of frog Sundays to do a job.

"I can't cut a stick on my whole piece 'cause Ged claims he'll have a right to replevin an equal number of sticks cut, if the surveyors back up his contention. Nasty mess. The original line was run years and years ago, and they're not many alive today in the Big woods that know the rights of it.

"I expect," added Uncle Henry, shaking his bushy head, "that old Toby Vanderwiller knows the rights of that line business; but he won't tell. Gedney Raffer's got a strangle hold on Toby and his little swamp farm, and Toby doesn't dare say his soul's his own. "Well!" continued the lumberman, with another of his big laughs. "This has nothing to do with your stew, Bob. I didn't want to come to the house last night and surprise you; so I stayed at the hotel. And all the time I was thinking of this little nip, Beg pardon! This young lady, and how smart and plucky she was.

"And lo and behold," pursued Uncle Henry, "she turns out to be my own niece. I'm going to take her back with me to Pine Camp. Kate's got to see and know her. The boys will be tickled out of their boots to have a girl like her around. That's our one lack at Pine Camp. There never was a girl in the family.

"Seems that this was just foreordained. You and Jessie have got to go 'way off, over the water; can't leave this plucky girl alone. Her old uncle and aunt are the proper folks to take care of her. What do you say yourself, young lady?"

Nan had liked the big man from the very beginning. She was a sensible child, too. She saw that she must settle this matter herself, for it was too hard a question for either Momsey or Papa Sherwood to decide. She gained control of herself now; but nobody will ever know how much courage it took for her to say, promptly:

"Of course I will go home with you, Uncle Henry. It will be fun, I think, to go into the woods in the winter. And, and I can come right back as soon as Momsey and Papa Sherwood return from Scotland."

So it was settled, just like that. The rush in which both parties got under way on Monday made Nan's head whirl. Momsey was to buy a few necessary things in New York before she boarded the steamer. Nan had a plentiful supply of warm winter clothing, and she took a trunkful.

Mrs. Joyce was left to take a peep at the little, locked cottage on Amity Street, now and then. Nan could say "Goodbye" only very hastily to Bess Harley and her other school friends. Her school had to be broken off at a bad time in the year, but there was the prospect of a change in Nan's method of education the next fall.

Momsey and Papa Sherwood took the train east an hour before Nan and Uncle Henry boarded that for Chicago. All went with a rush and clatter, and Nan found herself at last rumbling out of Tillbury, on her way to the northern wilderness, while a thin drive of fine snowflakes tapped on the car windows.

CHAPTER X
GEDNEY RAFFER

It was fortunate for Nan Sherwood that on the day of parting with her parents she had so much to do, and that there was so much to see, and so many new things of which to think.

She had never traveled to Chicago before, nor far from Tillbury at all. Even the chair car was new to the girl's experience and she found it vastly entertaining to sit at a broad window with her uncle in the opposite chair, gazing out upon the snowy landscape as the train hurried over the prairie.

She had a certain feeling that her Uncle Henry was an anomaly in the chair car. His huge bearskin coat and the rough clothing under it; his felt boots, with rubber soles and feet; the fact that he wore no linen and only a string tie under the collar of his flannel shirt; his great bronzed hands and blunted fingers with their broken nails, all these things set him apart from the other men who rode in the car.

Papa Sherwood paid much attention to the niceties of dress, despite the fact that his work at the Atwater Mills had called for overalls and, frequently, oily hands. Uncle Henry evidently knew little about stiff collars and laundered cuffs, or cravats, smart boots, bosomed shirts, or other dainty wear for men. He was quite innocent of giving any offence to the eye, however. Lying back in the comfortable chair with his coat off and his great lumberman's boots crossed, he laughed at anything Nan said that chanced to be the least bit amusing, until the gas-globes rang again.

It seemed to Nan as though there never was such a huge man before. She doubted if Goliath could have looked so big to young David, when the shepherd boy went out with his sling to meet the giant. Uncle Henry was six feet, four inches in height and broad in proportion. The chair creaked under his weight when he moved. Other people in the car gazed on the quite unconscious giant as wonderingly as did Nan herself.

"Uncle Henry," she asked him once, "are all the men in the Big Woods as tall as you are?"

"Goodness me! No, child," he chuckled. "But the woods don't breed many runts, that's a fact. There's some bigger than I. Long Sam Dorgan is near seven feet he isn't quite sure, for he's so ticklish that you can't ever measure him," and Uncle Henry's chuckle burst into a full-fledged laugh. "He's just as graceful as a length of shingle lathing, too. And freckles and liver spots on his hands and face, well, he certain sure is a handsome creature.

"He went to town once and stayed over night. Wasn't any bed long enough at the hotel, and Sam had got considerably under the weather, anyhow, from fooling with hard cider. So he wasn't particular about where he bedded down, and they put him to sleep in the horse trough."

"The horse trough!" gasped Nan.

"Yes. It was pretty dry when Sam went to bed; but right early in the morning a sleepy hostler stumbled out to the trough and began to pump water into it for the cattle. Maybe Long Sam needed a bath, but not just that way. He rose up with a yell like a Choctaw Indian. Said he was just dreaming of going through the Sault Ste. Marie in a barrel, and he reckoned the barrel burst open."

Nan was much amused by this story, as she was by others that the old lumberman related. He was full of dry sayings and his speech had many queer twists to it. His bluff, honest way delighted the girl, although he was so different from Papa Sherwood. As Momsey had said, Uncle Henry's body had to be big to contain his heart. One can excuse much that is rough in a character so lovable as that of Uncle Henry's.

The snow increased as the train sped on and the darkness gradually thickened. Uncle Henry took his niece into the dining car where they had supper, with a black man with shiny eyes and very white teeth, who seemed always on the broad grin, to wait upon them. Nan made a mental note to write Bess Harley all about the meal and the service, for Bess was always interested in anything that seemed "aristocratic," and to the unsophisticated girl from Tillbury the style of the dining car seemed really luxurious.

When the train rolled into the Chicago station it was not yet late; but it seemed to Nan as though they had ridden miles and miles, through lighted streets hedged on either side with brick houses. The snow was still falling, but it looked sooty and gray here in the city. Nan began to feel some depression, and to remember more keenly that Momsey and Papa Sherwood were flying easterly just as fast as an express train could take them.

It was cold, too. A keen, penetrating wind seemed to search through the streets. Uncle Henry said it came from the lake. He beckoned to a taxicab driver, and Nan's trunk was found and strapped upon the roof. Then off they went to the hotel where Uncle Henry always stopped when he came to Chicago, and where his own bag was checked.

Looking through the cab windows, the girl began to take an immediate interest in life again. So many people, despite the storm! So many vehicles tangled up at the corners and waiting for the big policemen to let them by in front of the clanging cars! Bustle, hurry, noise, confusion!

"Some different from your Tillbury," drawled Uncle Henry. "And just as different from Pine Camp as chalk is from cheese."

"But so interesting!" breathed Nan, with a sigh. "Doesn't it ever get to be bedtime for children in the city?"

"Not for those kids," grumbled Uncle Henry. "Poor creatures. They sell papers, or flowers, or matches, or what-not, all evening long. And stores keep open, and hotel bars, and drug shops, besides theatres and the like. There's a big motion picture place! I went there once. It beats any show that ever came to Hobart Forks, now I tell you."

"Oh, we have motion picture shows at Tillbury. We have had them in the school hall, too," said Nan complacently. "But, of course, I'd like to see all the people and the lights, and so forth. It looks very interesting in the city. But the snow is dirty, Uncle Henry."

"Yes. And most everything else is dirty when you get into these brick and mortar tunnels. That's what I call the streets. The air even isn't clean," went on the lumberman. "Give me the woods, with a fresh wind blowing, and the world looks good to me," then his voice and face fell, as he added, "excepting that snake-in-the-grass, Ged Raffer."

"That man must make you a lot of trouble, Uncle Henry," said Nan sympathetically.

"He does," growled the lumberman. "He's a miserable, fox-faced scoundrel, and I've no more use for him than I have for an egg-sucking dog. That's the way I feel about it."

They reached the hotel just then, and Uncle Henry's flare of passion was quenched. The hostelry he patronized was not a new hotel; but it was a very good one, and Nan's heart beat high as she followed the porter inside, with Uncle Henry directing the taxicab driver and a second porter how to dispose of the trunk for the night.

Nan had her bag in which were her night clothes, toilet articles, and other necessities. The porter carried this for her and seated her on a comfortable lounge at one side while Uncle Henry arranged about the rooms.

To do honor to his pretty niece the lumberman engaged much better quarters than he would have chosen for himself. When they went up to the rooms Nan found a pretty little bath opening out of hers, and the maid came and asked her if she could be of any help. The girl began to feel quite "grown up." It was all very wonderful, and she loved Uncle Henry for making things so pleasant for her.

She had to run to his door and tell him this before she undressed. He had pulled off his boots and was tramping up and down the carpeted floor in his thick woolen socks, humming to himself.

"Taking a constitutional, Nan," he declared. "Haven't had any exercise for this big body of mine all day. Sitting in that car has made me as cramped as a bear just crawling out of his den in the spring."

He did not tell her that had he been alone he would have gone out and tramped the snowy streets for half the night. But he would not leave her alone in the hotel. "No, sir," said Uncle Henry. "Robert would never forgive me if anything happened to his honey-bird. And fire, or something, might break out here while I was gone."

He said nothing like this to Nan, however, but kissed her good night and told her she should always bid him good night in just that way as long as she was at Pine Camp.

"For Kate and I have never had a little girl," said the big lumberman, "and boys get over the kissing stage mighty early, I find. Kate and I always did hanker for a girl."

"If you owned a really, truly daughter of your own, Uncle Henry, I believe you'd spoil her to death!" cried Nan, the next morning, when she came out of the fur shop to which he had taken her.

He had insisted that she was not dressed warmly enough for the woods. "We see forty and forty-five below up there, sometimes," he said. "You think this raw wind is cold; it is nothing to a black frost in the Big Woods. Trees burst as if there were dynamite in 'em. You've never seen the like.

"Of course the back of winter's about broken now. But we may have some cold snaps yet. Anyhow, you look warmer than you did."

And that was true, for Nan was dressed like a little Esquimau. Her coat had a pointed hood to it; she wore high fur boots, the fur outside. Her mittens of seal were buttoned to the sleeves of her coat, and she could thrust her hands, with ordinary gloves on them, right into these warm receptacles.

Nan thought they were wonderfully served at the hotel where they stopped, and she liked the maid on her corridor very much, and the boy who brought the icewater, too. There really was so much to tell Bess that she began to keep a diary in a little blank-book she bought for that purpose.

Then the most wonderful thing of all was the message from Papa Sherwood which arrived just before she and Uncle Henry left the hotel for the train. It was a "night letter" sent from Buffalo and told her that Momsey was all right and that they both sent love and would telegraph once more before their steamship left the dock at New York.

Nan and Uncle Henry drove through the snowy streets to another station and took the evening train north. They traveled at first by the Milwaukee Division of the Chicago and Northwestern Railroad; and now another new experience came Nan's way. Uncle Henry had secured a section in the sleeping car and each had a berth.

It was just like being put to sleep on a shelf, Nan declared, when the porter made up the beds at nine o'clock. She climbed into the upper berth a little later, sure that she would not sleep, and intending to look out of the narrow window to watch the snowy landscape fly by all night.

And much to her surprise (only the surprise came in the morning) she fell fast asleep almost immediately, lulled by the rocking of the huge car on its springs, and did not arouse until seven o'clock and the car stood on the siding in the big Wisconsin city.

They hurried to get a northern bound train and were soon off on what Uncle Henry called the "longest lap" of their journey. The train swept them up the line of Lake Michigan, sometimes within sight of the shore, often along the edge of estuaries, particularly following the contour of Green By, and then into the Wilderness of upper Wisconsin and the Michigan Peninsula.

On the Peninsula Division of the C. & N. W. they did not travel as fast as they had been running, and before Hobart Forks was announced on the last local train they traveled in, Nan Sherwood certainly was tired of riding by rail. The station was in Marquette County, near the Schoolcraft line. Pine Camp was twenty miles deeper in the Wilderness. It seemed to Nan that she had been traveling through forests, or the barren stumpage where forests had been, for weeks.

"Here's where we get off, little girl," Uncle Henry said, as he seized his big bag and her little one and made for the door of the car. Nan ran after him in her fur clothing. She had found before this that he was right about the cold. It was an entirely different atmosphere up here in the Big Woods from Tillbury, or even Chicago.

The train creaked to a stop. They leaped down upon the snowy platform. Only a plain station, big freight house, and a company of roughly dressed men to meet them. Behind the station a number of sleighs and sledges stood, their impatient horses shaking the innumerable bells they wore.

Nan, stumbling off the car step behind her uncle, came near to colliding with a small man in patched coat and cowhide boots, and with a rope tied about his waist as some teamsters affect. He mumbled something in anger and Nan turned to look at him.

He wore sparse, sandy whiskers, now fast turning gray. The outthrust of the lower part of his face was as sharp as that of a fox, and he really looked like a fox. She was sure of his identity before uncle Henry wheeled and, seeing the man, said:

"What's that you are saying, Ged Raffer? This is my niece, and if you lay your tongue to her name, I'll give you something to go to law about in a hurry. Come, Nan. Don't let that man touch so much as your coat sleeve. He's like pitch. You can't be near him without some of his meanness sticking to you."

CHAPTER XI
PINE CAMP AT LAST

It was the first shade upon Uncle Henry's character that displeased Nan. He was evidently a passionate man, prone to give way to elemental feelings, literally, "a man of wrath."

Gedney Raffer, weazened, snakelike, sly, and treacherous, had doubtless wronged Uncle Henry deeply. But this fact could not excuse the huge lumberman's language on the platform of the Hobart Forks station.

Nan wanted to stop her ears with her fingers and run from the spot. The tough fellows standing around enjoyed the war of words hugely. Mr. Sherwood was too big to strike Gedney Raffer, and of course the latter dared not use his puny fists on the giant.

The blunt club of the lumberman's speech was scarcely a match for the sharp rapier of Raffer's tongue. As the crowd laughed it was evident that the fox-faced man was getting the verbal best of the controversy.

Nan's ears burned and tears stood in her eyes. Uncle Henry descended to personal threats and the smaller man called out:

"You jest put your hand on me, you big, overgrown sawney! That's all I'm a-waitin' for. You 'tack me and I'll have you in the caboose, sure's my name's Gedney Raffer. Try it!"

The quarrel was most distressing. Nan pulled at her uncle's coat sleeve. The rough men eyed her curiously. She had never felt so ashamed in her life.

"Do come, Uncle Henry," she whispered. "I'm cold."

That statement started the fuming giant at once. Nan's sensitiveness to a rude quarrel did not impress the man; but her sensitiveness to the weather shocked him immediately.

"My goodness, girl! We'll go right up to the hotel," he said, kindly. "Any of you fellows seen Rafe or Tom in town this morning with the sled and roans?"

"Hey, Hen!" cried the station master, waving a yellow paper. "Here's a telegraph despatch for you."

It was really for Nan, and from Papa Sherwood filed just before the Afton Castle sailed from New York:

"Momsey and papa send love and kisses. Be cheerful and good. Write often. We think of you always. Kind wishes for Henry, Kate and boys. We look forward to fair voyage and safe landing. Will cable from other side. Expect happy meeting in spring. R. and J. Sherwood."

"They got a good start," commented Uncle Henry, putting all thought of his quarrel with Ged Raffer behind him at once. "We'll hope they have a safe voyage. Now! Where are those boys of mine?"

The town of Hobart Forks was by no means a lumber town. Millions of feet of timber was boomed on the river within the limits of the town every season, and there were great mills along the banks of the stream, too. But there were other industries, as well as churches, amusement places and many pleasant dwellings. It was no settlement of "slab shanties" with a few saloons and a general store. Nan had yet to see this latter kind of settlement.

But what she saw about the central market place of Hobart Forks opened her eyes considerably to an appreciation of the rough country she had come to, and the rough people to be met therein.

The storekeepers she saw through the frosted windows were dressed like storekeepers in Tillbury; and there were well dressed women on the streets, a few, at least.

But most of the men striding through the snow were as roughly dressed as her uncle, and not many were as good looking as Mr. Sherwood. Some who came out of the swinging doors of saloons staggered, and were very noisy in their speech and rude in their actions. Of course nobody spoke to Nan, or troubled her; Henry Sherwood was undoubtedly a man of standing in the settlement and highly respected.

Not far from the market place they came upon a sprawling old tavern, with a fenced yard at one side. As they approached, a sled drawn by a wild looking pair of rough, red-roan ponies, dashed out of the yard and stopped at the broad front portico of the hotel.

"Hey, Tom! What's the matter with you?" called Uncle Henry. "Here we are!"

The driver turned a broad, good-humored face to look over his burly shoulder. Nan saw that Tom Sherwood strongly resembled his father.

"That you, Dad?" he drawled. "I'd about given you up. I didn't want to drive down to the depot with these crazy creatures. And if I'd left 'em standing they'd have kicked Phil's shed to pieces, I do believe. The train's been in half an hour and more."

"I know," said his father. "I had a mess of words with Ged Raffer. That delayed me."

"You ought to give him the back of your hand, and say no more about it," declared Tom, in a tone that showed he warmed in his bosom the family grudge against the fox-faced man.

"Here's your Cousin Nan, Tom," said his father, without making rejoinder to the young man's observation. "She must go into Phil's and get warm and have a cup of hot coffee. I'll take some in a new-fangled bottle I bought down in Chicago, so we can all have a hot drink on the way home."

"'Twon't keep warm twenty miles," said Tom.

"Yes 'twill. It'll keep HOT for twenty miles and more. They call it a thermos bottle. It'll keep coffee hot, or cold, for a day, just as you please."

"Jehosaphat, Dad! What kind of a swindle's that? How does the bottle know whether you want your drink hot or cold? Huh! Those city folks couldn't make me believe any such thing," objected the son.

Nan had to giggle at that, and Uncle Henry demanded: "Did you ever see such a gump? Go on down to the station and tell Abe to fling that trunk and the bags into the back of the sled. We'll have our coffee, and get the thermos bottle filled, too, by the time you come back."

Nan liked tom Sherwood. He was about nineteen and almost as big as his father. He was gentle with her, and showed himself to be an expert driver of the roan colts. Otherwise Nan might have been much afraid during the first mile of the journey to Pine Camp, for certainly she had never seen horses behave so before.

"Haven't been out of the stable for a week," explained Tom cooly as the roans plunged and danced, and "cut up didos" generally, as Uncle Henry remarked.

"We had a big fall of snow," Tom went on to say. "Bunged us all up in the woods; so Rafe and I came in. Marm's all right. So's everybody else around the Camp, except Old Man Llewellen. He's down with rheumatism, or tic-douloureux, or something. He's always complaining."

"I know," said Uncle Henry, and then went on to relate for his son's benefit the wonderful thing that had happened to his brother and his brother's wife, and why Nan had come up into Michigan without her parents.

"We'll be mighty proud to have her," said Tom simply. He was only a great boy, after all, and he blushed every time he caught Nan looking at him. The girl began to feel very much grown up.

They were glad of the hot coffee, and Tom was shown how and why the mysterious bottle kept the drink hot. They only made that single halt (and only for a few minutes for the horses to drink) before reaching Pine Camp. They traveled through the snow-covered woods most of the way. There were few farms and no settlements at all until they reached Pine Camp.

The road was not well beaten and they could not have got through some of the drifts with less spirited ponies than the roans. When they crossed the long bridge over the river and swept into the village street, Nan was amazed.

Likewise, her heart sank a little. There was not a building in the place more than a story and a half in height. Most of them were slab cottages. Few yards were fenced. There were two stores, facing each other on the single street of the town, with false-fronts running up as tall as the second story would have been had there been a second story.

The roans dashed through the better beaten path of the street, with everybody along the way hailing Henry Sherwood vociferously. The giant waved his hand and shouted in reply. Nan cowered between him and Tom, on the seat, shielding her face from the flying snow from the ponies' hoofs, though the tears in her eyes were not brought there only by the sting of the pelting she received.

CHAPTER XII
"HOME WAS NEVER LIKE THIS"

The roan ponies dashed through the slab settlement, past the blacksmith and wheelwright shop and the ugly red building Tom told Nan was the school, and reached a large, sprawling, unpainted dwelling on the outskirts of the village.

There were barns back of the Sherwood house; there was no fence between the yard and the road, the windows of the house stared out upon the passerby, blindless, and many of them without shades. There was such a painful newness about the building that it seemed to Nan the carpenters must have just packed their tools and gone, while the painters had not yet arrived.

"Well! Here we are," announced Mr. Henry Sherwood, as Tom held in the still eager ponies. He stepped out and offered Nan his hand. "Home again, little girl. I reckon Kate will be mighty glad to see you, that she will."

Nan leaped out and began to stamp her feet on the hard snow, while Uncle Henry lifted out the trunk and bags. Just as the ponies sprang away again, a door in the ugly house opened and a tall, angular woman looked forth.

"Bring her in, Hen!" she cried, in a high-pitched voice. "I want to see her."

Nan went rather timidly up the path. Her aunt was almost as tall as her husband. She was very bony and was flat-chested and unlovely in every way. That is, so it seemed, when the homesick girl raised her eyes to Aunt Kate's face.

That face was as brown as sole-leather, and the texture of the skin seemed leathery as well. There was a hawklike nose dominating the unfeminine face. The shallows below the cheekbones were deep, as though she had suffered the loss of her back molars. The eyebrows were straggly; the eyes themselves of a pale, watery blue; the mouth a thin line when her colorless lips were closed; and her chin was as square and determined as Uncle Henry's own.

As Nan approached she saw something else about this unlovely woman. On her neck was a great, livid scar, of a hand's breadth, and which looked like a scald, or burn. No attempt was made to conceal this unsightly blemish.

Indeed, there was nothing about Aunt Kate Sherwood suggesting a softening of her hard lines. Her plain, ugly print dress was cut low at the throat, and had no collar or ruff to hide the scar. Nan's gaze was fastened on that blemish before she was half way to the door, and she could see nothing else at first.

The girl fought down a physical shudder when Aunt Kate's clawlike hands seized her by both shoulders, and she stooped to kiss the visitor.

"Welcome, dear Nannie," her sharp voice said, and Nan thought that, with ease, one might have heard her in the middle of the village.

But when Aunt Kate's lips touched the girl's forehead they were Warm, and soft as velvet. Her breath was sweet. There was a wholesome cleanliness about her person that pleased Nan. The ugly dress was spotless and beautifully laundered. She had a glimpse of the unplastered kitchen and saw a row of copper pots on the shelf over the dresser that were scoured to dazzling brightness. The boards of the floor were white as milk. The big, patent range glistened with polish, and its nickel-work was rubbed till it reflected like a mirror.

"Welcome, my dear!" said Aunt Kate again. "I hope you will be happy while you stay with us."

Happy! With Momsey and Papa Sherwood on the ocean, and the "little dwelling in amity" closed and deserted? Nan feared she would break down and cry.

Her Aunt Kate left her to herself a minute just then that she might overcome this weakness. Uncle Henry came up the path with the bags, smiling broadly.

"Well, old woman!" he said heartily.

"Well, old man!" she returned.

And then suddenly, Nan Sherwood had a new vision. She was used to seeing her pretty mother and her handsome father display their mutual affection; it had not seemed possible that rough, burly Uncle Henry and ugly Aunt Kate could feel the same degree of affection for each other.

Uncle Henry dropped the bags. Aunt Kate seemed to be drawn toward him when he put out his hands. Nan saw their lips meet, and then the giant gently, almost reverently, kissed the horrid scar on Aunt Kate's neck.

"Here's Nan!" cried the big lumberman jovially. "The pluckiest and smartest little girl in seven states! Take her in out of the cold, Kate. She's not used to our kind of weather, and I have been watching for the frost flowers to bloom on her pretty face all the way from the forks."

The woman drew Nan into the warm kitchen. Uncle Henry followed in a minute with the trunk.

"Where'll I put this box, Kate?" he asked. "I reckon you've fixed up some cozy place for her?"

"The east room, Hen," Aunt Kate replied. "The sun lies in there mornings. I took the new spring rocker out of the parlor, and with the white enameled bedstead you bought in Chicago, and the maple bureau we got of that furniture pedlar, and the best drugget to lay over the carpet I reckon Nannie has a pretty bedroom."

Meanwhile Nan stared openly around the strange kitchen. The joists and rafters were uncovered by laths or plaster. Muslin, that had once been white, was tacked to the beams overhead for a ceiling. The smoke from the cookstove had stained it to a deep brown color above the stove and to a lighter, meerschaum shade in the corners.

The furniture was of the rudest plainest kind much of it evidently home-made. Uncle Henry was not unhandy with tools. She learned, later, that he and the boys had practically built the house by themselves. They were finishing it inside, as they had time. In some of the rooms the inside window and door frames were not yet in place.

There was an appetizing smell from the pots upon the stove, and the long table was set for dinner. They would not let Nan change from her traveling dress before sitting down to the table. Tom and Rafe came in and all three men washed at the long, wooden sink.

Rafe was of slighter build than his brother, and a year or more younger. He was not so shy as Tom, either; and his eyes sparkled with mischief. Nan found that she could not act "grown up" with her Cousin Rafe.

The principal dish for dinner was venison stew, served with vegetables and salt-rising bread. There was cake, too, very heavy and indigestible, and speckled with huckleberries that had been dried the fall previous. Aunt Kate was no fancy cook; but appetite is the best sauce, after all, and Nan had her share of that condiment.

During the meal there was not much conversation save about the wonderful fortune that had fallen to Nan's mother and the voyage she and her husband were taking to Scotland to secure it. Nan learned, too, that Uncle Henry had telegraphed from Tillbury of Nan's coming to Pine Camp, and consequently Aunt Kate was able to prepare for her.

And that the good woman had done her best to make a nest for her little niece in the ugly house, Nan was assured. After dinner she insisted upon the girl's going to the east room to change her dress and lie down. The comparison between this great chamber and Nan's pretty room at home was appalling.

The room had been plastered, but the plaster was of a gray color and unfinished. The woodwork was painted a dusty, brick red with mineral paint. The odd and ugly pieces of furniture horrified Nan. The drugget on the floor only served to hide a part of the still more atrociously patterned carpet. The rocking chair complained if one touched it. The top of the huge maple dresser was as bald as one's palm.

Nan sat down on the unopened trunk when her aunt had left her. She dabbed her eyes with her handkerchief. Home certainly was never like this! She did not see how she was ever going to be able to stand it.

CHAPTER XIII
MARGARET LLEWELLEN

"If Momsey or Papa Sherwood knew about this they'd be awfully sorry for me," thought Nan, still sitting on the trunk. "Such a looking place! Nothing to see but snow and trees," for the village of Pine Camp was quite surrounded by the forest and all the visitor could see from the windows of her first-floor bedroom were stumps and trees, with deep snow everywhere.

There was a glowing wood stove in the room and a big, chintz-covered box beside it, full of "chunks." It was warm in the room, the atmosphere being permeated with the sweet tang of wood smoke.

Nan dried her eyes. There really was not any use in crying. Momsey and Papa Sherwood could not know how bad she felt, and she really was not selfish enough to wish them to know.

"Now, Nanny Sherwood!" she scolded herself, "there's not a particle of use of your sniveling. It won't 'get you anywhere,' as Mrs. Joyce says. You'll only make your eyes red, and the folks will see that you're not happy here, and they will be hurt.

"Mustn't make other folks feel bad just because I feel bad myself," Nan decided. "Come on! Pluck up your courage!

"I know what I'll do," she added, literally shaking herself as she jumped off the trunk. "I'll unpack. I'll cover up everything ugly that I can with something pretty from Tillbury."

Hurried as she had been her departure from the cottage on Amity Street, Nan had packed in her trunk many of those little possessions, dear to her childish heart, that had graced her bedroom. These appeared from the trunk even before she hung away her clothes in the unplastered closet where the cold wind searched through the cracks from out-of-doors. Into that closet, away back in the corner, went a long pasteboard box, tied carefully with strong cord. Nan patted it gently with her hand before she left the box, whispering:

"You dear! I wouldn't have left you behind for anything! I won't let them know you are here; but sometimes, when I'm sure nobody will interrupt, you shall come out."

She spread a fringed towel over the barren top of the dresser. It would not cover it all, of course; but it made an island in a sea of emptiness.

And on the island she quickly set forth the plain little toilet-set her mother had given her on her last birthday, the manicure set that was a present from Papa Sherwood, and the several other knickknacks that would help to make the big dresser look as though "there was somebody at home," as she whispered to herself.

She draped a scarf here, hung up a pretty silk bag there, placed Momsey's and Papa Sherwood's portraits in their little silver filigree easels on the mantelpiece, flanking the clock that would not run and which was held by the ugly china shepherdess with only one foot and a broken crook, the latter ornament evidently having been at one time prized by the babies of her aunt's family, for the ring at the top was dented by little teeth.

Nothing, however, could take the curse of ugliness off the staring gray walls of the room, or from the horrible turkey-red and white canton-flannel quilt that bedecked the bed. Nan longed to spill the contents of her ink bottle over that hideous coverlet, but did not dare.

The effort to make the big east room look less like a barn made Nan feel better in her mind. It was still dreary, it must be confessed. There were a dozen things she wished she could do to improve it. There were nothing but paper shades at the windows. Even a simple scrim curtain— — -

And, in thinking of this, Nan raised her eyes to one window to see a face pressed close against the glass, and two rolling, crablike eyes glaring in at her.

"Mercy!" ejaculated Nan Sherwood. "What is the matter with that child's eyes? They'll drop out of her head!"

She ran to the window, evidently startling the peeper quite as much as she had been startled herself. The girl, who was about Nan's own age, fell back from the pane, stumbled in the big, men's boots she wore, and ungracefully sprawled in the snow upon her back. She could not get away before Nan had the window open.

The sash was held up by a notched stick. Nan put her head and shoulders out into the frosty air and stared down at the prostrate girl, who stared up at her in return.

"What do you want?" Nan asked.

"Nothin'," replied the stranger.

"What were you peeping in for?"

"To see you," was the more frank reply.

"What for?" asked Nan.

"Ain't you the new gal?"

"I've newly come here, yes," admitted Nan.

"Well!"

"But I'm not such a sight, am I?" laughed the girl from Tillbury. "But you are, lying there in the snow. You'll get your death of cold. Get up."

The other did so. Beside the men's boots, which were patched and old, she wore a woollen skirt, a blouse, and a shawl over her head and shoulders. She shook the snow from her garments much as a dog frees himself from water after coming out of a pond.

"It's too cold to talk with this window open. You're a neighbor, aren't you?"

The girl nodded.

"Then come in," urged Nan. "I'm sure my aunt will let you."

The girl shook her head in a decided negative to this proposal. "Don't want Marm Sherwood to see me," she said.

"Why not?"

"She told me not to come over after you come 'ithout I put on my new dress and washed my hands and face."

"Well!" exclaimed Nan, looking at her more closely. "You seem to have a clean face, at least."

"Yes. But that dress she 'gin me, my brother Bob took and put on Old Beagle for to dress him up funny. And Beagle heard a noise he thought was a fox barking and he started for the tamarack swamp, lickety-split. I expect there ain't enough of that gingham left to tie around a sore thumb."

Nan listened to this in both amusement and surprise. The girl was a new specimen to her.

"Come in, anyway," she urged. "I can't keep the window open."

"I'll climb in, then," declared the other suddenly, and, suiting the action to the word, she swarmed over the sill; but she left one huge boot in the snow, and Nan, laughing delightedly, ran for the poker to fish for it, and drew it in and shut down the window.

The strange girl was warming her hands at the fire. Nan pushed a chair toward her and took one herself, but not the complaining spring rocking chair.

"Now tell me all about yourself," the girl demanded.

"I'm Nan Sherwood, and I've come here to Pine Camp to stay while my father and mother have gone to Scotland."

"I've heard about Scotland," declared the girl with the very prominent eyes.

"Have you?"

"Yes. Gran'ther Llewellen sings that song. You know:

"'Scotland's burning! Scotland's burning! Where, where? Where, where? Fire! Fire! Fire! Fire! Pour on water! Pour on water! Fire's out! Fire's out!'"

Nan laughed. "I've heard that, too," she said. "But it was another Scotland." Then: "So your name is Llewellen?"

"Marg'ret Llewellen."

"I've heard your grandfather is sick," said Nan, remembering Tom's report of the health of the community when he had met her and her uncle at Hobart Forks.

"Yes. He's got the tic-del-rew," declared Margaret, rather unfeelingly. "Aunt Matildy says he's allus creakin' round like a rusty gate-hinge."

"Why! That doesn't sound very nice," objected Nan. "Don't you love your grandfather?"

"Not much," said this perfectly frank young savage. "He's so awfully wizzled."

"'Wizzled'?" repeated Nan, puzzled.

"Yes. His face is all wizzled up like a dried apple."

"But you love your aunt Matilda?" gasped Nan.

"Well, she's wizzled some," confessed Margaret. Then she said: "I don't like faces like hern and Marm Sherwood's. I like your face. It's smooth."

Nan had noticed that this half-wild girl was of beautifully fair complexion herself, and aside from her pop eyes was quite petty. But she was a queer little thing.

"You've been to Chicago, ain't you?" asked Margaret suddenly.

"We came through Chicago on our way up here from my home. We stayed one night there," Nan replied.

"It's bigger'n Pine Camp, ain't it?"

"My goodness, yes!"

"Bigger'n the Forks?" queried Margaret doubtfully.

"Why, it is much, much bigger," said Nan, hopeless of making one so densely ignorant understand anything of the proportions of the metropolis of the lakes.

"That's what I told Bob," Margaret said. "He don't believe it. Bob's my brother, but there never was such a dunce since Adam."

Nan had to laugh. The strange girl amused her. But Margaret said something, too, that deeply interested the visitor at Pine Camp before she ended her call, making her exit as she had her entrance, by the window.

"I reckon you never seen this house of your uncle's before, did you?" queried Margaret at one point in the conversation.

"Oh, no. I never visited them before."

"Didn't you uster visit 'em when they lived at Pale Lick?"

"No. I don't remember that they ever lived anywhere else beside here."

"Yes, they did. I heard Gran'ther tell about it. But mebbe 'twas before you an' me was born. It was Pale Lick, I'm sure. That's where they lost their two other boys."

"What two other boys?" asked Nan, amazed.

"Didn't you ever hear tell you had two other cousins?"

"No," said Nan.

"Well, you did," said Margaret importantly. "And when Pale Lick burned up, them boys was burned up, too."

"Oh!" gasped Nan, horrified.

"Lots of folks was burned. Injun Pete come near being burned up. He ain't been right, I reckon, since. And I reckon that's where Marm Sherwood got that scar on the side of her neck."

Nan wondered.

CHAPTER XIV
AT THE LUMBER CAMP

Nan said nothing just then about her queer little visitor. Aunt Kate asked her when she came out of the east room and crossed the chill desert of the parlor to the general sitting room:

"Did you have a nice sleep, Nannie?"

"Goodness, Auntie!" laughed Nan. "I got over taking a nap in the daytime a good while ago, I guess. But you come and see what I have done. I haven't been idle."

Aunt Kate went and peeped into the east chamber. "Good mercy, child! It doesn't look like the same room, with all the pretty didos," she said. "And that's your pretty mamma in the picture on the mantel? My! Your papa looks peaked, doesn't he? Maybe that sea voyage they are taking will do 'em both good."

Nan had to admit that beside her uncle and cousins her father did look "peaked." Robust health and brawn seemed to be the two essentials in the opinion of the people of Pine Camp. Nan was plump and rosy herself and so escaped criticism.

Her uncle and aunt, and the two big boys as well, were as kind to her as they knew how to be. Nan could not escape some of the depression of homesickness during the first day or two of her visit to the woods settlement; but the family did everything possible to help her occupy her mind.

The long evenings were rather amusing, although the family knew little about any game save checkers, "fox and geese," and "hickory, dickory, dock." Nan played draughts with her uncle and fox and geese and the other kindergarten game with her big cousins. To see Tom, with his eyes screwed up tight and the pencil poised in his blunt, frost-cracked fingers over the slate, while he recited in a base sing-song:

"Hick'ry, dick'ry, dock
The mouse ran up the clock,
The clock struck one,

An' down he come

Hick'ry, dick'ry, dock,"

was side-splitting. Nan laughed till she cried. Poor, simple Tom did know just what amused his little cousin so.

Rafe was by no means so slow, or so simple. Nan caught him cheating more than once at fox and geese. Rafe was a little sly, and he was continually making fun of his slow brother, and baiting him. Uncle Henry warned him:

"Now, Rafe, you're too big for your Marm or me to shingle your pants; but Tom's likely to lick you some day for your cutting up and I sha'n't blame him. Just because he's slow to wrath, don't you get it in your head that he's afraid, or that he can't settle your hash in five minutes."

Nan was greatly disturbed to hear so many references to fistic encounters and fighting of all sorts. These men of the woods seemed to be possessed of wild and unruly passions. What she heard the boys say caused her to believe that most of the spare time of the men in the lumber camps was spent in personal encounters.

"No, no, deary. They aren't so bad as they sound," Aunt Kate told her, comfortably. "Lots of nice men work in the camps all their lives and never fight. Look at your Uncle Henry."

But Nan remembered the "mess of words" (as he called it) that Uncle Henry had had with Gedney Raffer on the railroad station platform at the Forks, and she was afraid that even her aunt did not look with the same horror on a quarrel that Nan herself did.

The girl from Tillbury had a chance to see just what a lumber camp was like, and what the crew were like, on the fourth day after her arrival at her Uncle Henry's house. The weather was then pronounced settled, and word came for the two young men, Tom and Rafe, to report at Blackton's camp the next morning, prepared to go to work. Tom drove a team which was then at the lumber camp, being cared for by the cook and foreman; Rafe was a chopper, for he had that sleight with an ax which, more than mere muscle, makes the mighty woodsman.

"Their dad'll drive 'em over to Blackton's early, and you can go, too," said Aunt Kate. "That is, if you don't mind getting up right promptly in the morning?"

"Oh, I don't mind that," Nan declared. "I'm used to getting up early."

But she thought differently when Uncle Henry's heavy hand rapped on the door of the east chamber so early the next morning that it seemed to Nan Sherwood that she had only been in bed long enough to close her eyes.

"Goodness, Uncle!" she muttered, when she found out what it meant. "What time is it?"

"Three o'clock. Time enough for you to dress and eat a snack before we start," replied her uncle.

"Well!" said Nan to herself. "I thought the house was afire."

Uncle Henry heard her through the door and whispered, shrilly: "Sh! Don't let your aunt hear you say anything like that, child."

"Like what?" queried Nan, in wonder.

"About fire. Remember!" added Uncle Henry, rather sternly, Nan thought, as he went back to the kitchen.

Then Nan remembered what the strange little girl, Margaret Llewellen, had said about the fire at Pale Lick that had burned her uncle's former home. Nan had not felt like asking her uncle or aunt, or the boys, either, about it. The latter had probably been too young to remember much about the tragedy.

Although Nan had seen Margaret on several fleeting occasions since her first interview with the woods girl, there had been no opportunity of talking privately with her. And Margaret would only come to the window. She was afraid to tell "Marm Sherwood" how she had lost the new dress that had been given to her.

It was now as black outside Nan's window as it could be. She lit her oil lamp and dressed swiftly, running at last through the cold parlor and sitting room into the kitchen, where the fire in the range was burning briskly and the coffee pot was on. Tom and Rafe were there comfortably getting into thick woolen socks and big lumbermen's boots.

There was a heaping pan of Aunt Kate's doughnuts on the table, flanked with the thick china coffee cups and deep saucers. Her uncle and the boys always poured their coffee into the saucers and blew on it to take the first heat off, then gulped it in great draughts.

Nan followed suit this morning, as far as cooling the coffee in the saucer went. There was haste. Uncle Henry had been up some time, and now he came stamping into the house, saying that the ponies were hitched in and were standing in readiness upon the barn floor, attached to the pung.

"We've twenty-five miles to ride, you see, Nannie," he said. "The boys have to be at Blackton's so's to get to work at seven."

They filled the thermos bottle that had so puzzled Tom, and then sallied forth. The ponies were just as eager as they had been the day Nan had come over from the Forks. She was really half afraid of them.

It was so dark that she could scarcely see the half-cleared road before them as the ponies dashed away from Pine Camp. The sky was completely overcast, but Uncle Henry declared it would break at sunrise.

Where the track had been well packed by former sleighs, the ponies' hoofs rang as though on iron. The bits of snow that were flung off by their hoofs were like pieces of ice. The bells on the harness jingled a very pretty tune, Nan thought. She did not mind the biting cold, indeed, only her face was exposed. Uncle Henry had suggested a veil; but she wanted to see what she could.

For the first few miles it remained very dark, however. Had it not been for the snow they could not have seen objects beside the road at all. There was a lantern in the back of the pung and that flung a stream of yellow light behind them; but Uncle Henry would not have the radiance of it shot forward.

"A light just blinds you," he said. "I'd rather trust to the roans' sense."

The ponies galloped for a long way, it seemed to Nan; then they came to a hill so steep that they were glad to drop to a walk. Their bodies steamed in a great cloud as they tugged the sleigh up the slope. Dark woods shut the road in on either hand. Nan's eyes had got used to the faint light so that she could see this at least.

Suddenly she heard a mournful, long-drawn howl, seemingly at a great distance.

"Must be a farm somewhere near," she said to Rafe, who sat beside her on the back seat.

"Nope. No farms around here, Nan," he returned.

"But I hear a dog howl," she told him.

Rafe listened, too. Then he turned to her with a grin on his sharp face that she did not see. "Oh, no, you don't," he chuckled. "That's no dog."

Again the howl was repeated, and it sounded much nearer. Nan realized, too, that it was a more savage sound than she had ever heard emitted by a dog.

"What is it?" she asked, speaking in a low voice to Rafe.

"Wolves!" responded her cousin maliciously. "But you mustn't mind a little thing like that. You don't have wolves down round where you live, I s'pose?"

Nan knew that he was attempting to plague her, so she said: "Not for pets, at least, Rafe. These sound awfully savage."

"They are," returned her cousin calmly.

The wolf cry came nearer and nearer. The ponies had started on a trot again at the top of the hill, and her uncle and Tom did not seem to notice the ugly cry. Nan looked back, and was sure that some great animal scrambled out of the woods and gave chase to them.

"Isn't there some danger?" she asked Rafe again.

"Not for us," he said. "Of course, if the whole pack gathers and catches us, then we have to do something."

"What do you do?" demanded Nan quickly.

"Why, the last time we were chased by wolves, we happened to have a ham and a side of bacon along. So we chucked out first the one, and then the other, and so pacified the brutes till we got near town."

"Oh!" cried Nan, half believing, half in doubt.

She looked back again. There, into the flickering light of the lantern, a gaunt, huge creature leaped. Nan could see his head and shoulders now and then as he plunged on after the sleigh, and a wickeder looking beast, she hoped never to see.

"Oh!" she gasped again, and grabbed at Rafe's arm.

"Don't you be afraid," drawled that young rascal. "I reckon he hasn't many of his jolly companions with him. If he had, of course, we'd have to throw you out to pacify him. That's the rule—youngest and prettiest goes first— —-"

"Like the ham, I s'pose?" sniffed Nan, in some anger, and just then Tom reached over the back of the front seat and seized his brother by the shoulder with a grip that made Rafe shriek with pain.

Nan was almost as startled as was Rafe. In the half-darkness Tom's dull face blazed with anger, and he held his writhing brother as though he were a child.

"You ornery scamp!" he said, almost under his breath. "You try to scare that little girl, and I'll break you in two!"

Nan was horrified. She begged Tom to let his brother alone. "I was only fooling her," snarled Rafe, rubbing his injured shoulder, for Tom had the grip of a pipe wrench.

Uncle Henry never turned around at all; but he said: "If I had a gun I'd be tempted to shoot that old wolf hound of Toby Vanderwiller's. He's always running after sleds and yelling his head off."

Nan was glad the creature following them was not really a wolf; but she knew she should be just as much afraid of him if she met him alone, as though he really were a wolf. However, mostly, she was troubled by the passionate nature of her two cousins. She had never seen Tom show any anger before; but it was evident that he had plenty of spirit if it were called up. And she was, secretly, proud that the slow-witted young giant should have displayed his interest in her welfare so plainly. Rafe sat and nursed his shoulder in silence for several miles.

The cold was intense. As the sky lightened along the eastern horizon it seemed to Nan as though the frost increased each moment. The bricks at their feet were getting cool; and they had already had recourse to the thermos bottle, which was now empty of the gratefully hot drink it had contained.

As the light gradually increased Nan saw Rafe watching her with sudden attention. After his recent trick she was a little afraid of Rafe. Still it did not seem possible that the reckless fellow would attempt any second piece of fooling so soon after his brother's threat.

But suddenly Rafe yelled to his father to pull down the roans, and as the ponies stopped, he reached from the sled into a drift and secured a big handful of snow. Seizing Nan quickly around the shoulders he began to rub her cheek vigorously with the snow. Nan gasped and almost lost her breath; but she realized immediately what Rafe was about.

The frost had nipped her cheek, and her cousin had seen the white spot appear. "The rubbing stung awfully, and the girl could not keep back the tears; but she managed to repress the sobs.

"There!" exclaimed Rafe. "You are a plucky girl. I'm sorry I got some of that snow down your neck, Nan. Couldn't help it. But it's the only thing to do when the thermometer is thirty-two degrees below zero. Why! A fellow went outside with his ears uncovered at Droomacher's camp one day last winter and after awhile he began to rub his ears and one of 'em dropped off just like a cake of ice."

"Stop your lying, boy!" commanded his father. "It isn't as bad as that, Nan. But you want to watch out for frost bite here in the woods, just the same as we had to watch out for the automobiles in crossing those main streets in Chicago."

With a red sun rising over the low ridge of wooded ground to the east, the camp in the hollow was revealed, the smoke rising in a pillar of blue from the sheet-iron chimney of the cookhouse; smoke rising, too, from a dozen big horses being curried before the stables.

Most of the men had arrived the night before. They were tumbling out of the long, low bunkhouse now and making good use of the bright tin washbasins on the long bench on the covered porch. Ice had been broken to get the water that was poured into the basins, but the men laved their faces and their hairy arms and chests in it as though it were summer weather.

They quickly ran in for their outer shirts and coats, however, and then trooped in to the end of the cook shed where the meals were served. Tom turned away to look over his horses and see that they were all ready for the day's work. Rafe put up the roan ponies in a couple of empty stalls and gave them a feed of oats.

Uncle Henry took Nan by the hand, and, really she felt as though she needed some support, she was so stiff from the cold, and led her into the warm room where the men were gathering for the hearty meal the cook and his helper had prepared.

The men were boisterous in their greeting of Uncle Henry, until they saw Nan. Than, some bashfully, some because of natural refinement, lowered their voices and were more careful how they spoke before the girl.

But she heard something that troubled her greatly. An old, grizzled man in a corner of the fireplace where the brisk flames leaped high among the logs, and who seemed to have already eaten his breakfast and was busily stoning an axe blade, looked up as Nan and her uncle approached, saying:

"Seen Ged Raffer lately, Hen?"

"I saw him at the Forks the other day, Toby," Mr. Sherwood replied.

"Yaas. I heard about that," said the old man drawlingly. "But since then?"

"No."

"Wal, he was tellin' me that he'd got you on the hip this time, Hen. If you as much as put your hoof over on that track he's fighting you about, he'll plop you in jail, that's what he'll do! He's got a warrant all made out by Jedge Perkins. I seen it."

Uncle Henry walked closer to the old man and looked down at him from his great height. "Tobe," he said, "you know the rights of that business well enough. You know whether I'm right in the contention, or whether Ged's right. You know where the old line runs. Why don't you tell?"

"Oh, mercy me!" croaked the old man, and in much haste. "I ain't goin' to git into no land squabble, no, sir! You kin count me out right now!" And he picked up his axe, restored the whetstone to its sheath on the wall, and at once went out of the shack.

CHAPTER XV
A CAT AND HER KITTENS

That was a breakfast long to be remembered by Nan Sherwood, not particularly because of its quality, but for the quantity served. She had never seen men like these lumbermen eat before, save for the few days she had been at Uncle Henry's house.

Great platters of baked beans were placed on the table, flanked by the lumps of pork that had seasoned them. Fried pork, too, was a "main-stay" on the bill-of-fare. The deal table was graced by no cloth or napery of any kind. There were heaps of potatoes and onions fried together, and golden cornbread with bowls of white gravy to ladle over it.

After riding twenty-five miles through such a frosty air, Nan would have had to possess a delicate appetite indeed not to enjoy these viands. She felt bashful because of the presence of so many rough men; but they left her alone for the most part, and she could listen and watch.

"Old Toby Vanderwiller tell you what Ged's been blowin' about, Henry?" asked one of the men at the table, busy ladling beans into his mouth with a knife, a feat that Nan thought must be rather precarious, to say the least.

"Says he's going to jail me if I go on to the Perkins Tract," growled Uncle Henry, with whom the matter was doubtless a sore subject.

"Yaas. But he says more'n that," said this tale bearer.

"Oh, Ged says a whole lot besides his prayers," responded Uncle Henry, good-naturedly. Perhaps he saw they were trying to bait him.

"Wal, 'tain't nothin' prayerful he's sayin'," drawled the first speaker, after a gulp of coffee from his thick china cup. "Some of the boys at Beckett's, you know, they're a tough crowd, was riggin' him about what you said to him down to the Forks, and Ged spit out that he'd give a lump of money to see you on your back."

"Huh!" grunted Uncle Henry.

"And some of 'em took him up, got the old man right down to cases."

"That so?" asked Mr. Sherwood curiously. "What's Ged going to do? Challenge me to a game of cat's cradle? Or does he want to settle the business at draughts, three best out o' five?"

"Now you know dern well, Hen," said the other, as some of the listeners laughed loudly at Mr. Sherwood's sally, "that old Ged Raffer will never lock horns with you 'ceptin' it's in court, where he'll have the full pertection of the law, and a grain the best of it into the bargain."

"Well, I s'pose that's so," admitted Nan's uncle, rather gloomily, she thought.

"So, if Beckett's crowd are int'rested in bumping you a whole lot, you may be sure Ged's promised 'em real money for it."

"Pshaw!" exclaimed Uncle Henry. "You're fooling now. He hasn't hired any half-baked chip-eaters and Canucks to try and beat me up?"

"I ain't foolin'."

"Pshaw!"

"You kin 'pshaw' till the cows come home," cried the other heatedly. "I got it straight."

"Who from?"

"Sim Barkis, him what's cookin' for Beckett's crew."

"Good man, Sim. Never caught him in a lie yet. You are beginning to sound reasonable, Josh," and Mr. Sherwood put down his knife and fork and looked shrewdly at his informant. "Now tell me," he said, "how much is Sim going to get for helping to pay Ged Raffer's debts?"

"Har!" ejaculated the other man. "You know Sim ain't that kind."

"All right, then. How much does he say the gang's going to split between 'em after they've done me up brown according to contract?" scoffed Uncle Henry, and Nan realized that her giant relative had not the least fear of not being able to meet any number of enemies in the open.

"Sim come away before they got that far. Of course Ged didn't say right out in open meetin' that he'd give so many dollars for your scalp. But he got 'em all int'rested, and it wouldn't surprise him, so Sim said, if on the quiet some of those plug-uglies had agreed to do the job."

Nan shuddered, and had long since stopped eating. But nobody paid any attention to her at the moment.

Uncle Henry drawled: "They're going to do the hardest day's job for the smallest pay that they ever did on this Michigan Peninsula. I'm much obliged to you, Josh, for telling me. I never go after trouble, as you fellows all know; but I sha'n't try to dodge it, either."

He picked up his knife and fork and went quietly on with his breakfast. But Nan could not eat any more at all.

It seemed to the gently nurtured girl from Tillbury as though she had fallen in with people from another globe. Even the mill-hands, whom Bess Harley so scorned, were not like these great, rough fellows whose minds seemed continually to be fixed upon battle. At least, she had never seen or heard such talk as had just now come to her ears.

The men began, one by one, to push back the benches and go out. There was a great bustle of getting under way as the teams started for the woods, and the choppers, too, went away. Tom hurried to start his big pair of dapple grays, and Nan was glad to bundle up again and run out to watch the exodus.

They were a mighty crew. As Uncle Henry had said, the Big Woods did not breed runts.

Remembering the stunted, quick-moving, chattering French Canadians, and the scattering of American-born employees among them, who worked in the Tillbury mills, Nan was the more amazed by the average size of these workmen. The woodsmen were a race of giants beside the narrow-shouldered, flat-chested pygmies who toiled in the mills.

Tom strode by with his timber sled. Rafe leaped on to ride and Tom playfully snapped his whiplash at him. Nan was glad to see that the two brothers smiled again at each other. Their recent tiff seemed to be forgotten.

Some of the choppers had already gone on ahead to the part of the tract where the marked trees were being felled. Now the pluck, pluck, pluck of the axe blows laid against the forest monarchs, reached the girl's ears. She thought the flat stuttering sound of the axes said "pluck" very plainly, and that that was just the word they should say.

"For it does take lots of pluck to do work of this kind," Nan confided to her uncle, who walked up and down on the porch smoking an after-breakfast pipe.

"Yes. No softies allowed on the job," said he, cheerfully. "Some of the boys may be rough and hard nuts to crack; but it is necessary to have just such boys or we couldn't get out the timber."

"But they want to fight so much!" gasped Nan.

"Sho!" said her uncle, slowly. "It's mostly talk. They feel the itch for hard work and hard play, that's all. You take lively, full-muscled animals, and they are always bucking and quarreling—trying to see which one is the best. Take two young, fat steers they'll lock horns at the drop of a hat. It's animal spirits, Nan. They feel that they've got to let off steam. Where muscle and pluck count for what they do in the lumber camps, there's bound to be more or less ructions."

Perhaps this might be; but Nan was dreadfully sorry, nevertheless, that Uncle Henry had this trouble with Mr. Gedney Raffer. The girl feared that there had been something besides "letting off steam" in the challenge her uncle had thrown down to his enemy, or to the men that enemy could hire to attack him.

The timber sledges soon began to drift back, for some of the logs had been cut before the big storm, and had only to be broken out of the drifts and rolled upon the sleds with the aid of the men's canthooks. It was a mystery at first to Nan how they could get three huge logs, some of them three feet in diameter at the butt, on to the sled; two at the bottom and one rolled upon them, all being fastened securely with the timber-chain and hook.

How the horses strained in their collars to start the mighty load! But once started, the runners slipped along easily enough, even through the deep snow, packing the compressible stuff in one passage as hard as ice. Nan followed in this narrow track to the very bank of the river where the logs were heaped in long windrows, ready to be launched into the stream when the waters should rise at the time of the spring freshet.

Tom managed his team alone, and unloaded alone, too. It was marvelous (so Nan thought) that her cousin could start the top log with the great canthook, and guide it as it rolled off the sled so that it should lie true with timbers that had been piled before. The strain of his work made him perspire as though it were midsummer. He thrust the calks on his bootsoles into the log and the shreds of bark and small chips flew as he stamped to get a secure footing for his work. Then he heaved like a giant, his shoulders humping under the blue jersey he wore, and finally the log turned. Once started, it was soon rolled into place.

Nan ran into the cook shed often to get warm. Her uncle was busy with the boss of the camp, so she had nobody but the cook and his helper to speak to for a time. Therefore it was loneliness that made her start over the half-beaten trail for the spot where the men were at work, without saying a word to anybody.

None of the teams had come by for some time; but she could hear faintly the sound of the axes and the calling of the workmen to each other and their sharp commands to the horses.

She went away from the camp a few hundred yards and then found that the trail forked. One path went down a little hill, and as that seemed easy to descend, Nan followed it into a little hollow. It seemed only one sled had come this way and none of the men were here. The voices and axes sounded from higher up the ridge.

Suddenly she heard something entirely different from the noise of the woodsmen. It was the snarling voice of a huge cat and almost instantly Nan sighted the creature which stood upon a snow-covered rock beside the path. It had tasseled ears, a wide, wicked "smile," bristling whiskers, and fangs that really made Nan tremble, although she was some yards from the bobcat.

As she believed, from what her cousins had told her, bobcats are not usually dangerous. They never seek trouble with man, save under certain conditions; and that is when a mother cat has kittens to defend.

This was a big female cat, and, although the season was early, she had littered and her kittens, three of them, were bedded in a heap of leaves blown by the wind into a hollow tree trunk.

The timberman driving through the hollow had not seen the bobcat and her three blind babies; but he had roused the mother cat and she was now all ready to spring at intruders.

That Nan was not the person guilty of disturbing her repose made no difference to the big cat. She saw the girl standing, affrighted and trembling, in the path and with a ferocious yowl and leap she crossed the intervening space and landed in the snow within almost arm's reach of the fear-paralyzed girl.

CHAPTER XVI
"INJUN PETE"

Nan Sherwood could not cry out, though she tried. She opened her lips only to find her throat so constricted by fear that she could not utter a sound. Perhaps her sudden and utter paralysis was of benefit at the moment, after all; for she could not possibly have escaped the infuriated lynx by running.

The creature's own movements were hampered by the deep drift in which she had landed. The soft snow impeded the cat and, snarling still, she whirled around and around like a pinwheel to beat a firmer foundation from which to make her final spring at her victim.

Nan, crouching, put her mittened hands before her face. She saw no chance for escape and could not bear to see the vicious beast leap at her again. "Momsey! Papa Sherwood!" she thought, rather than breathed aloud.

Then, down the hill toward her, plunged a swift body. She rather felt the new presence than saw it. The cat yowled again, and spit. There was the impact of a clubbed gun upon the creature's head.

"Sacre bleu! Take zat! And zat!" cried a sharp voice, between the blows that fell so swiftly. The animal's cries changed instantly from rage to pain. Nan opened her eyes in time to see the maddened cat flee swiftly. She bounded to the big tree and scrambled up the trunk and out upon the first limb. There she crouched, over the place where her kittens were hidden, yowling and licking her wounds. There was blood upon her head and she licked again and again a broken forefoot between her yowls of rage and pain.

But Nan was more interested just then in the person who had flown to her rescue so opportunely. He was not one of the men from the camp, or anybody whom she had ever seen before.

He was not a big man, but was evidently very strong and active. His dress was of the most nondescript character, consisting mainly of a tattered fur cap, with a woolen muffler tied over his ears; a patched and parti-colored coat belted at the waist with a frayed rope. His legs disappeared into the wide tops of a pair of boots evidently too big for him, with the feet bundled in bagging so that he could walk on top of the snow, this in lieu of regular snowshoes.

His back was toward Nan and he did not turn to face her as he said:

"Be not afeared, leetle Man'zelle. Le bad chat is gone. We shall now do famous-lee, eh? No be afeared more."

"No, no, sir," gasped Nan, trying to be brave. "Won't, won't it come back?"

"Nev-air!" cried the man, with a flourish of the gun which was a rusty-barreled old weapon, perhaps more dangerous at the butt end than at its muzzle. "Ze chat only fear for her babies. She have zem in dat tree. We will go past leeving zem streectly alone, eh?"

"No!" cried Nan hastily. "I'm going back to the camp. I didn't know there were such dangerous things as that in these woods."

"Ah! You are de strange leetle Mam'zelle den?" responded the man. "You do not know ze Beeg Woods?"

"I guess I don't know anything about this wilderness," confessed Nan. "My uncle brought me to the camp up yonder this morning, and I hope he'll go right home again. It's awful!"

"Eet seem terrifying to ze leetle Mam'zelle because she is unused—eh? Me! I be terrified at ze beeg city where she come from, p'r'aps. Zey tell Pete 'bout waggings run wizout horses, like stea'mill. Ugh! No wanter see dem. Debbil in 'em," and he laughed, not unpleasantly, making a small joke of the suggestion.

Indeed his voice, now that the sharpness of excitement had gone out of it, was a very pleasant voice. The broken words he used assured Nan that his mother tongue must be French. He was probably one of the "Canucks" she had heard her cousins speak of. French Canadians were not at all strange to Nan Sherwood, for in Tillbury many of the mill hands were of that race.

But she thought it odd that this man kept his face studiously turned from her. Was he watching the bobcat all the time? Was the danger much more serious than he would own?

"Why don't you look at me?" cried the girl, at length. "I'm awfully much obliged to you for coming to help me as you did. And my uncle will want to thank you I am sure. Won't you tell me your name?"

The man was silent for a moment. Then, when he spoke, his voice was lower and there was an indescribably sad note in it.

"Call me 'Injun Pete', zat me. Everybody in de beeg Woods know Injun Pete. No odder name now. Once ze good Brodders at Aramac goin' make scholar of Pete, make heem priest, too, p'r'aps. He go teach among he's mudder's people. Mudder Micmac, fadder wild Frinchman come to dees lakeshore. But nev-air can Pete be Teacher, be priest. Non, non! Jes' Injun Pete."

Nan suddenly remembered what little Margaret Llewellen had said about the fire at Pale Lick, and "Injun Pete." The fact that this man kept his face turned from her all this time aroused her suspicion. She was deeply, deeply grateful to him for what he had just done for her, and, naturally, she enlarged in her mind the peril in which she had been placed.

Margaret had suggested this unfortunate half-breed was "not right in his head" because of the fire which had disfigured him. But he spoke very sensibly now, it seemed to Nan; very pitifully, too, about his blasted hopes of a clerical career. She said, quietly:

"I expect you know my uncle and his family, Pete. He is Mr. Sherwood of Pine Camp."

"Ah! Mis-tair Hen Sherwood! I know heem well," admitted the man. "He nice-a man ver' kind to Injun Pete."

"I'd like to have you look at me, please," said Nan, still softly. "You see, I want to know you again if we meet. I am very grateful."

Pete waved her thanks aside with a royal gesture. "Me! I be glad to be of use, oh, oui! Leetle Man'zelle mus' not make mooch of nottin', eh?"

He laughed again, but he did not turn to look at her. Nan reached out a tentative hand and touched his sleeve. "Please, Mr. Pete," she said. "I, I want to see you. I, I have heard something about your having been hurt in a fire. I am sure you must think yourself a more hateful sight than you really are."

A sob seemed to rise in the man's throat, and his shoulders shook. He turned slowly and looked at her for a moment over his shoulder. Then he went swiftly away across the snow (for the bobcat had disappeared into her lair) and Nan stumbled back up the trail toward the camp, the tears blinding her own eyes.

The disfigured face of the half-breed HAD been a shock to her. She could never speak of it afterward. Indeed, she could not tell Uncle Henry about her meeting with the lynx, and her rescue—she shrank so from recalling Injun Pete's disfigured face.

CHAPTER XVII
SPRING IN THE BIG WOODS

That visit to the lumber camp was memorable for Nan Sherwood in more ways than one. Her adventure with the lynx she kept secret from her relatives, because of the reason given in the previous chapter. But there was another incident that marked the occasion to the girl's mind, and that was the threat of Gedney Raffer, reported to her Uncle Henry.

Nan thought that such a bad man as Raffer appeared to be would undoubtedly carry out his threat. He had offered money to have Mr. Sherwood beaten up, and the ruffians he had bribed would doubtless be only too eager to earn the reward.

To tell the truth, for weeks thereafter, Nan never saw a rough-looking man approach the house on the outskirts of Pine Camp, without fearing that here was coming a ruffian bent on her uncle's injury.

That Uncle Henry seemed quite to have forgotten the threat only made Nan more keenly alive to his danger. She dared not discuss the matter with Aunt Kate, for Nan feared to worry that good woman unnecessarily. Besides, having been used to hiding from her own mother all unpleasant things, the girl naturally displayed the same thoughtfulness for Aunt Kate.

For, despite Mrs. Henry Sherwood's bruskness and masculine appearance, Nan learned that there were certain matters over which her aunt showed extreme nervousness.

For instance, she was very careful of the lamps used in the house—she insisted upon cleaning and caring for them herself; she would not allow a candle to be used, because it might be overturned; and she saw to it herself that every fire, even the one in Nan's bedroom, was properly banked before the family retired at night.

Nan had always in mind what Uncle Henry said about mentioning fire to Aunt Kate; so the curious young girl kept her lips closed upon the subject. But she certainly was desirous of knowing about that fire, so long ago, at Pale Lick, how it came about; if Aunt Kate had really got her great scar there; and if it was really true that two members of her uncle's family had met their death in the conflagration.

She tried not to think at all of Injun Pete. That was too terrible!

With all her heart, Nan wished she might do something that would really help Uncle Henry solve his problem regarding the timber rights on the Perkins Tract. The very judge who had granted the injunction forbidding Mr. Sherwood to cut timber on the tract was related to the present owners of the piece of timberland; and the tract had been the basis of a feud in the Perkins family for two generations.

Many people were more or less interested in the case and they came to the Sherwood home and talked excitedly about it in the big kitchen. Some advised an utter disregard of the law. Others were evidently minded to increase the trouble between Raffer and Uncle Henry by malicious tale-bearing.

Often Nan thought of what Uncle Henry had said to old Toby Vanderwiller. She learned that Toby was one of the oldest settlers in this part of the Michigan Peninsula, and in his youth had been a timber runner, that is, a man who by following the surveyors' lines on a piece of timber, and weaving back and forth across it, can judge its market value so nearly right that his employer, the prospective timber merchant, is able to bid intelligently for the so-called "stumpage" on the tract.

Toby was still a vigorous man save when that bane of the woodsman, rheumatism, laid him by the heels. He had a bit of a farm in the tamarack swamp. Once, being laid up by his arch enemy, with his joints stiffened and muscles throbbing with pain, Toby had seen the gaunt wolf of starvation, more terrible than any timber wolf, waiting at his doorstone. His old wife and a crippled grandson were dependent on Toby, too.

Thus in desperate straits Toby Vanderwiller had accepted help from Gedney Raffer. It was a pitifully small sum Raffer would advance upon the little farm; but it was sufficient to put Toby in the usurer's power. This was the story Nan learned regarding Toby. And Uncle Henry believed that Toby, with his old-time knowledge of land-boundaries, could tell, if he would, which was right in the present contention between Mr. Sherwood and Gedney Raffer.

These, and many other subjects of thought, kept the mind of Nan Sherwood occupied during the first few weeks of her sojourn at Pine Camp. She had, too, to keep up her diary that she had begun for Bess Harley's particular benefit. Every week she sent off to Tillbury a bulky section of this report of her life in the Big woods. It was quite wonderful how much there proved to be to write about. Bess wrote back, enviously, that never did anything interesting, by any possibility, happen, now that Nan was away from Tillbury. The town was "as dull as ditch water." She, Bess, lived only in hopes of meeting her chum at Lakeview Hall the next September.

This hope Nan shared. But it all lay with the result of Momsey's and Papa Sherwood's visit to Scotland and Emberon Castle. And, Nan thought, it seemed as though her parents never would even reach that far distant goal.

They had taken a slow ship for Momsey's benefit and the expected re-telegraphed cablegram was looked for at the Forks for a week before it possibly could come.

It was a gala day marked on Nan's calendar when Uncle Henry, coming home from the railroad station behind the roan ponies, called to her to come out and get the message. Momsey and Papa Sherwood had sent it from Glasgow, and were on their way to Edinburgh before Nan received the word. Momsey had been very ill a part of the way across the ocean, but went ashore in improved health.

Nan was indeed happy at this juncture. Her parents were safely over their voyage on the wintry ocean, so a part of her worry of mind was lifted.

Meanwhile spring was stealing upon Pine Camp without Nan's being really aware of the fact. Uncle Henry had said, back in Chicago, that "the back of winter was broken"; but the extreme cold weather and the deep snow she had found in the Big Woods made Nan forget that March was passing and timid April was treading on his heels.

A rain lasting two days and a night washed the roads of snow and turned the fast disappearing drifts to a dirty yellow hue. In sheltered fence corners and nooks in the wood, the grass lifted new, green blades, and queer little Margaret Llewellen showed Nan where the first anemones and violets hid under last year's drifted leaves.

The river ice went out with a rush after it had rained a few hours; after that the "drives" of logs were soon started. Nan went down to the long, high bridge which spanned the river and watched the flood carry the logs through.

At first they came scatteringly, riding the foaming waves end-on, and sometimes colliding with the stone piers of the bridge with sufficient force to split the unhewn timbers from end to end, some being laid open as neatly as though done with axe and wedge.

When the main body of the drive arrived, however, the logs were like herded cattle, milling in the eddies, stampeded by a cross-current, bunching under the bridge arches like frightened steers in a chute. And the drivers herded the logs with all the skill of cowboys on the range.

Each drive was attended by its own crew, who guarded the logs on either bank, launching those that shoaled on the numerous sandbars or in the shallows, keeping them from piling up in coves and in the mouths of estuaries, or creeks, some going ahead at the bends to fend off and break up any formation of the drifting timbers that promised to become a jam.

Behind the drive floated the square bowed and square sterned chuck-boat, which carried cook and provisions for the men. A "boom", logs chained together, end to end, was thrown out from one shore of the wide stream at night, and anchored at its outer end. Behind this the logs were gathered in an orderly, compact mass and the men could generally get their sleep, save for the watchman; unless there came a sudden rise of water in the night.

It was a sight long to be remembered, Nan thought, when the boom was broken in the morning. Sometimes an increasing current piled the logs up a good bit. It was a fear-compelling view the girl had of the river on one day when she went with Uncle Henry to see the first drive from Blackton's camp. Tom was coming home with his team and was not engaged in the drive. But reckless Rafe was considered, for his age, a very smart hand on a log drive.

The river had risen two feet at the Pine Camp bridge overnight. It was a boiling brown flood, covered with drifting foam and debris. The roar of the freshet awoke Nan in her bed before daybreak. So she was not surprised to see the river in such a turmoil when, after a hasty breakfast, she and Uncle Henry walked beside the flood.

"They started their drive last night," Uncle Henry said, "and boomed her just below the campsite. We'll go up to Dead Man's Bend and watch her come down. There is no other drive betwixt us and Blackton's."

"Why is it called by such a horrid name, Uncle?" asked Nan.

"What, honey?" he responded.

"That bend in the river."

"Why, I don't know rightly, honey-bird. She's just called that. Many a man's lost his life there since I came into this part of the country, that's a fact. It's a dangerous place," and Nan knew by the look on her uncle's face that he was worried.

CHAPTER XVIII
AT DEAD MAN'S BEND

Nan and her uncle came out on the bluff that overlooked the sharp bend which hid the upper reaches of the river from Pine Camp. Across the stream, almost from bank to bank, a string of gravel flats made a barrier that all the rivermen feared.

Blackton was no careless manager, and he had a good foreman in Tim Turner. The big boss had ridden down to the bend in a mud-splashed buggy, and was even prepared to take a personal hand in the work, if need be. The foreman was coming down the river bank on the Pine Camp side of the stream, watching the leading logs of the drive, and directing the foreguard. Among the latter Nan spied Rafe.

"There he is, Uncle!" she cried. "Oh! He's jumped out on that log, see?"

"He's all right, girl, he's all right," said Uncle Henry comfortingly. "Rafe's got good calks on his boots."

The boy sprang from log to log, the calks making the chips fly, and with a canthook pushed off a log that had caught and swung upon a small bank. He did it very cleverly, and was back again, across the bucking logs, in half a minute.

Below, the foreman himself was making for a grounded log, one of the first of the drive. It had caught upon some snag, and was swinging broadside out, into the stream. Let two or three more timbers catch with it and there would be the nucleus of a jam that might result in much trouble for everybody.

Tim Turner leaped spaces of eight and ten feet between the logs, landing secure and safe upon the stranded log at last. With the heavy canthook he tried to start it.

"That's a good man, Tim Turner," said Mr. Sherwood, heartily. "He's worked for me, isn't afraid of anything, Ha! But that's wrong!" he suddenly exclaimed.

Turner had failed to start the stranded log. Other logs were hurtling down the foam-streaked river, aimed directly for the stranded one. They would begin to pile up in a heap in a minute. The foreman leaped to another log, turning as he did so to face the shore. That was when Uncle Henry declared him wrong.

Turner was swinging his free arm, and above the roar of the river and the thunder of the grinding and smashing logs they could hear him shouting for somebody to bring him an axe. One of his men leaped to obey. Nan and Mr. Sherwood did not notice just then who this second man was who put himself in jeopardy, for both had their gaze on the foreman and that which menaced him.

Shooting across on a slant was a huge log, all of three feet through at the butt, and it was aimed for the timber on which Turner stood. He did not see it. Smaller logs were already piling against the timber he had left, and had he leaped back to the stranded one he would have been comparatively safe.

Mr. Sherwood was quick to act in such an emergency as this; but he was too far from the spot to give practical aid in saving Turner from the result of his own heedlessness. He made a horn of his two hands and shouted to the foreguard at the foot of the bluff:

"He's going into the water! Launch Fred Durgin's boat below the bend! Get her! Quick, there!"

Old riverman that he was, Uncle Henry was pretty sure of what was about to happen. The huge log came tearing on, butt first, a wave of troubled water split by its on-rush. Turner was watching the person bringing him the axe, and never once threw a glance over his shoulder.

Suddenly Nan cried out and seized Uncle Henry's arm. "Look! Oh, Uncle! It's Rafe!" she gasped, pointing.

"Aye, I know it," said her uncle, wonderfully cool, Nan thought, and casting a single glance at the figure flying over the bucking logs toward the endangered foreman. "He'll do what he can."

Nan could not take her eyes from her cousin after that. It seemed to be a race between Rafe and the charging log, to see which should first reach the foreman. Rafe, reckless and harebrained as he was, flew over the logs as sure-footed as a goat. Nan felt faint. Her cousin's peril seemed far greater to her than that of the foreman.

A step might plunge Rafe into the foaming stream! When a log rolled under him she cried out under her breath and clamped her teeth down on to her lower lip until the blood almost came.

"He'll be killed! He'll be killed!" she kept repeating in her own mind. But Uncle Henry stood like a rock and seemingly gave no more attention to his son than he did to Turner, or to the men running down the bank to seize upon and launch the heavy boat.

Rafe was suddenly balked and had to stop. Too great a stretch of water separated him from the next floating log. Turner beckoned him on. It was difficult to make the foreman hear above the noise of the water and the continual grinding of the logs, but Rafe yelled some warning and pointed toward the timber now almost upon Turner's foothold.

The man shot a glance behind him. The butt of the driving log rose suddenly into the air as though it would crush him.

Turner leaped to the far end of the log on which he stood. But too great a distance separated him from the log on which Rafe had secured a foothold.

Crash!

Nan heard, on top of the bluff, the impact of the great timber as it was flung by the current across the smaller log. Turner shot into the air as though he were flung from a catapult. But he was not flung in Rafe's direction, and the boy could not help him.

He plunged into the racing stream and disappeared. The huge timber rode over the smaller log and buried it from sight. But its tail swung around and the great log was headed straight down the river again.

As its smaller end swung near, Rafe leaped for it and secured a footing on the rolling, plunging log. How he kept his feet under him Nan could not imagine. A bareback rider in a circus never had such work as this. Rafe rode his wooden horse in masterly style.

There, ahead of him in the boiling flood, an arm and head appeared. Turner came to the surface with his senses unimpaired and he strove to clutch the nearest log. But the stick slipped away from him.

Rafe ran forward on the plunging timber he now rode the huge stick that had made all the trouble, and tried to reach the man in the water. No use!

Of course, there was no way for Rafe to guide his log toward the drowning man. Nor did he have anything to reach out for Turner to grasp. The axe handle was not long enough, and the foreman's canthook had disappeared.

Below, the men were struggling to get the big boat out from under the bank into the stream. Two of them stood up with their canthooks to fend off the drifting logs; the others plied the heavy oars.

But the boat was too far from the man in the river. He was menaced on all sides by plunging logs. He barely escaped one to be grazed on the shoulder by another. A third pressed him under the surface again; but as he went down this second time, Rafe Sherwood threw away his axe and leaped into the flood!

CHAPTER XIX
OLD TOBY VANDERWILLER

Nan was sure her Cousin Rafe would be drowned, as well as his foreman. She covered her eyes for a moment, and could not look.

Then a great cheer arose from the men in the boat and those still remaining on the bank of the river. Her uncle, beside her, muttered:

"Plucky boy! Plucky boy!"

Her eyes flew open and she looked again. In the midst of the scattering foam she saw a small log over which her cousin had flung his left arm; his other arm was around the foreman, and Rafe was bearing his head above water. Turner had been struck and rendered senseless by the blow.

The small log slipped through a race between two shallows, ahead of the greater timber. The latter indeed grounded for a moment and that gave the victim of the accident and his rescuer a chance for life.

They shot ahead with the log to which Rafe clung. The men in the boat shouted encouragement, and rowed harder. In a minute the boat came alongside the log and two of the rivermen grabbed the boy and the unconscious foreman. They had them safely in the boat, and the boat was at the shore again in three minutes.

By that time the big boss himself, Mr. Blackton, was tearing out over the logs from the other shore, axe in hand, to cut the key log of the jam, the formation of which Turner had tried to prevent. A hundred logs had piled up against the stoppage by this time and there promised to be a bad time at the bend if every one did not work quickly.

Before Nan and her uncle could reach the foot of the bluff, Turner had regained consciousness and was sitting on a stranded log, holding his head. Rafe, just as he had come out of the river, was out on the logs again lending a hand at the work so necessary to the success of the drive.

"Oh, dear me!" cried Nan, referring to her cousin, "he ought to go home and change his clothes. He'll get his death of cold."

"He'll work hard enough for the next hour to overcome the shock of the cold water. It's lucky if he isn't in again before they get that trouble over," responded Uncle Henry. Then he added, proudly: "That's the kind of boys we raise in the Big Woods, Nannie. Maybe they are rough-spoken and aren't really parlor-broke, but you can depend on 'em to do something when there's anything to do!"

"Oh, Uncle!" cried the girl. "I think Rafe is just the bravest boy I ever saw. But I should think Aunt Kate would be scared every hour he is away from home, he is so reckless."

She was very proud herself of Rafe and wrote Bess a lot about him. Slow Tom did not figure much in Nan Sherwood's letters, or in her thoughts, about this time. Thoughts and letters were filled with handsome Rafe.

It was while the Blackton drive was near Pine Camp that Nan became personally acquainted with old Toby Vanderwiller. It was after dinner that day that she met Margaret and Bob Llewellen and the three went down to the river bank, below the bridge, to watch the last of the Blackton drive.

The chuck-boat had pushed off into the rough current and was bobbing about in the wake of the logs; but all the men had not departed.

"That's old Toby," said Bob, a black-haired boy, full of mischief. "He don't see us. Le's creep up and scare him."

"No," said Nan, decidedly; "don't you dare!"

"Aw, shucks! Girls ain't no fun," the boy growled. "Mag's bad enough, but you air wuss'n she, Nan Sherwood. What's old Toby to you? He's allus as cross as two sticks, anyway."

"We won't make him any crosser," said Nan, laughing. "What's the good?"

Nan saw that the old man had his coat off, and had slipped down the right sleeve of his woolen shirt to bare his shoulder and upper right arm. He was clumsily trying to bandage the arm.

"He's got hurt," Nan cried to Margaret. "I wonder how?"

"Dunno," returned the smaller girl, carelessly. Although she was not mischievous like her brother, Margaret seldom showed traits of tenderness or affection. Nan was in some doubt as to whether the strange girl liked her. Margaret often patted Nan's cheeks and admired her smooth skin; but she never expressed any real affection. She was positively the oddest little piece of humanity Nan had ever met.

Once Nan asked her if she had a doll. "Doll?" snarled Margaret with surprising energy. "A'nt Matildy give me one once't an' I throwed it as far as I could inter the river, so I did! Nasty thing! Its face was all painted and rough."

Nan could only gasp. Drown a doll-baby! Big girl as she considered herself, she had a very tender spot in her heart for doll-babies.

Margaret Llewellen only liked people with fair faces and smooth complexions; she could not possibly be interested in old Toby Vanderwiller, who seemed always to need a shave, and whose face, like that of Margaret's grandfather, was "wizzled."

Nan ran down to him and asked: "Can't I help you, Mr. Vanderwiller? Did you get badly hurt?"

"Hullo!" grunted Toby. "Ain't you Hen Sherwood's gal?"

"I'm his niece," she told him. "Can I help?"

"Well, I dunno. I got a wallop from one o' them logs when we was breakin' that jam, and it's scraped the skin off me arm— —"

"Let me see," cried Nan, earnestly. "Oh! Mr. Vanderwiller! That must be painful. Haven't you anything to put on it?"

"Nothin' but this rag," grunted Toby, drily. "An' ye needn't call me 'Mister,' Sissy. I ain't useter bein' addressed that way."

Nan laughed; but she quickly washed the scraped patch on the old man's arm with clean water and then bound her own handkerchief over the abrasion under the rather doubtful rag that Toby himself supplied.

"You're sure handy, Sissy," he said, rising and allowing her to help him into the shirt again and on with his coat. "Now I'll hafter toddle along or Tim will give me a call-down. Much obleeged. If ye get inter the tam'rack swamp, come dry-foot weather, stop and see me an' my old woman."

"Oh! I'd love to, Mr. Vanderwiller," Nan cried. "The swamp must be full of just lovely flowers now."

The old man's face wrinkled into a smile, the first she had seen upon it. Really! He was not a bad looking man, after all.

"You fond of posies, sissy?" he asked.

"Indeed I am!" she cried.

"There's a-plenty in the swamp," he told her. "And no end of ferns and sich. You come see us and my old woman'll show ye. She's a master hand at huntin' up all kind o' weeds I tell her."

"I'll surely come, when the weather gets warmer," Nan called after Toby as the old man dogtrotted down the bank of the river. But he did not answer and was quickly out of sight.

CHAPTER XX
NAN'S SECRET

But Margaret Llewellen declared she would not go with her!

"It's nasty in the Tam'rack swamp; and there's frogs and, and snakes. Ketch me! And as fur goin' ter see Tobe and his old woman, huh! They're both as ugly as sin."

"Why, Margaret!" exclaimed Nan, in horror. "How you talk!"

"Wal, it's so. I don't like old, wizzled-up folks, I don't, now I tell ye!"

"That sounds awfully cruel," said Nan, soberly.

"Huh!" snorted Margaret, no other word would just express her manner of showing disgust. "There ain't no reason why I should go 'round makin' believe likin' them as I don't like. Dad useter take the hide off'n me and Bob for lyin'; an' then he'd stand an' palaver folks that he jest couldn't scurce abide, fur I heard him say so. That's lyin', too ain't it?"

"I, I don't believe it is right to criticize our parents," returned Nan, dodging the sharp girl's question.

"Mebbe yourn don't need criticizin'," responded Margaret, bluntly. "My dad ain't no angel, you kin bet."

And it was a fact that the Llewellen family was a peculiar one, from "Gran'ther" down to Baby Bill, whom Margaret did not mind taking care of when he was not "all broke out with the rash on his face." The girl's dislike for any countenance that was not of the smoothest, or skin of the softest texture, seemed strange indeed.

Margaret's mother was dead. She had five brothers and sisters of assorted ages, up to 'Lonzo, who was sixteen and worked in the woods like Nan's cousins.

Aunt Matilda kept house for the motherless brood, and for Gran'ther and Mr. Fen Llewellen. They lived in a most haphazard fashion, for, although they were not really poor, the children never seemed to have any decent clothing to wear; and if, by chance, they got a new garment, something always happened to it as, for instance, the taking of Margaret's new gingham by Bob as a dress for old Beagle.

As the Llewellens were close neighbors of the Sherwoods, Nan saw much of Margaret. The local school closed soon after the visitor had come to Pine Camp, and Nan had little opportunity of getting acquainted with other girls, save at the church service, which was held in the schoolhouse only every other Sunday. There was no Sunday School at Pine Camp, even for the very youngest of the children.

Nan talked to Aunt Kate about that. Aunt Kate was the very kindest-hearted woman that ever lived; but she had little initiative herself about anything outside her own house. "Goodness knows, I'd like to see the kiddies gathered together on Sunday afternoon and taught good things," she signed; "but lawsy, Nan! I'm not the one to do it. I'm not good enough myself."

"Didn't you teach Tom and Rafe, and—and—" Nan stopped. She had almost mentioned the two older boys of her aunt's, whom she had heard were destroyed in the Pale Lick fire. Aunt Kate did not notice, for she went on to say:

"Why—yes; I taught Tom and Rafe to say their prayers, and I hope they say 'em now, big as they are. And we often read the Bible. It's a great comfort, the main part of it. I never did take to the 'begats,' though."

"But couldn't we," suggested Nan, "interest other people and gather the children together on Sundays? Perhaps the old gentleman who comes here to preach every fortnight might help."

"Elder Posey's not here but three hours or so, any time. Just long enough to give us the word and grab a bite at somebody's house. Poor old man! He attends three meetings each Sunday, all different, and lives on a farm at Wingate weekdays where he has to work and support his family.

"He doesn't get but fifty dollars a year from each church, it's not making him a millionaire very fast," pursued Aunt Kate, with a soft little laugh. "Poor old man! I wish we could pay him more; but Pine Camp's not rich."

"You all seem to have enough and to spare, Auntie," said Nan, who was an observant girl for her age. "Nobody here is really poor."

"Not unless he's right down lazy," said her aunt, vigorously.

"Then I should think they'd build a proper church and give a minister some more money, so that he could afford to have a Sunday School as well."

"Lawsy me, Nan!" exclaimed her aunt. "The men here in Pine Camp haven't been woke up to such things. They hate to spend that fifty dollars for Elder Posey, they'd get a cheaper man if there were such. There's never been much out of the common happen here at Pine Camp. It takes trouble and destruction to wake folks up to their Christian duty in these woods. Now, at Pale Lick they've got a church— —-"

She stopped suddenly, and her face paled, while the ugly scar on her neck seemed to glow; but that may have been only in contrast. Aunt Kate turned away her head, and finally arose and went into her own room and closed the door. Nan dared not continue the subject when the good woman came out again, and the talk of a Sunday School for Pine Camp, for the time being, was ended.

There were hours when the girl from Tillbury was very lonely indeed. Writing to Bess and other girl friends in her old home town and penning long letters on thin paper to Momsey and Papa Sherwood in Scotland, did not fill all of these hours when Nan shut herself into that east room.

Sometimes she pulled down the paper shades and opened the clothes closet door, bringing out the long box she had hidden away there on the first day she had come to Pine Camp. In that box, wrapped in soft tissue paper, and dressed in the loveliest gown made by Momsey's own skillful fingers, was the great doll that had been given to Nan on her tenth birthday.

When girls went to high school, of course they were supposed to put away dolls, together with other childish things. But Nan Sherwood never could neglect her doll-babies and had often spent whole rainy days playing with them in secret in the attic of the little house on Amity Street.

Her other dolls had been left, carefully wrapped and shielded from the mice, at Tillbury; but Nan had been unable to leave Beautiful Beulah behind. She packed her in the bottom of her trunk, unknown even to Momsey in the hurry of departure. She had not told a soul here at Pine Camp that she possessed a doll; she knew the boys would make fun of her for sure.

But she often sat behind the drawn shades nursing the big doll and crooning softly to it as she swung back and forth in the spring rocking-chair. Tom had oiled the springs for her so that it no longer creaked.

She did not confide even in Aunt Kate about the big doll. They were all very kind to her; but Nan had a feeling that she ought to be grown up here among her backwoods relatives. How could she ever face roguish Rafe if he knew she liked to "play dolls?"

Fearing that even Margaret would tell, Nan had never shown the woods girl Beautiful Beulah. Once she was afraid Margaret had come to the window to peep in when Nan had the doll out of her hiding place; but she was not sure, and Nan hoped her secret was still inviolate. At least, Margaret never said a word about it.

Margaret's sisters had dolls made of corncobs, and rag babies with painted faces like the one Margaret had thrown into the river and drowned; but Margaret turned up her nose at them all. She never seemed to want to "play house" as do most girls of her age. She preferred to run wild, like a colt, with Bob in the woods and swamp.

Margaret did not wish to go into the swamp with Nan, however, on her first visit to Toby Vanderwiller's little farm. This was some weeks after the log drives, and lumbering was over for the season. Uncle Henry and the boys, rather than be idle, were working every acre they owned, and Nan was more alone than she had ever been since coming to Pine Camp.

She had learned the way to Toby's place, the main trail through the swamp going right by the hummock on which the old man's farm was situated. She knew there was a corduroy road most of the way—that is, a road built of logs laid side by side directly over the miry ground. Save in very wet weather this road was passable for most vehicles.

The distance was but three miles, however, and Nan liked walking. Besides, nobody who has not seen a tamarack swamp in late spring or early summer, can ever imagine how beautiful it is. Nan never missed human companionship when she was on the long walks she so often took in the woods.

She had learned now that, despite her adventure with the lynx in the snow-drifted hollow, there was scarcely any animal to fear about Pine Camp. Bears had not been seen for years; bobcats were very infrequently met with and usually ran like scared rabbits; foxes were of course shy, and the nearest approach to a wolf in all that section was Toby Vanderwiller's wolfhound that had once frightened Nan so greatly.

Hares, rabbits, squirrels, chipmunks, and many, many birds, peopled the forest and swamp. In sunken places where the green water stood and steamed in the sun, turtles and frogs were plentiful; and occasionally a snake, as harmless as it was wicked looking, slid off a water-soaked log at Nan's approach and slipped under the oily surface of the pool.

On the day Nan walked to Toby's place the first time, she saw many wonders of plant life along the way, exotics clinging to rotten logs and stumps; fronds of delicate vines that she had never before heard of; ferns of exquisite beauty. And flashing over them, and sucking honey from every cuplike flower, were shimmering humming-birds and marvelously marked butterflies.

The birds screamed or sang or chattered over the girl's head as she tripped along. Squirrels peeped at her, barked, and then whisked their tails in rapid flight. Through the cool, dark depths where the forest monarchs had been untouched by the woodsmen, great moths winged their lazy flight. Nan knew not half of the creatures or the wonderful plants she saw.

There were sounds in the deeps of the swamplands that she did not recognize, either. Some she supposed must be the voices of huge frogs; other notes were bird-calls that she had never heard before. But suddenly, as she approached a turn in the corduroy road, her ear was smitten by a sound that she knew very well indeed.

It was a man's voice, and it was not a pleasant one. It caused Nan to halt and look about for some place to hide until the owner of the voice went by. She feared him because of his harsh tones, though she did not, at the moment, suspect who it was.

Then suddenly she heard plainly a single phrase: "I'd give money, I tell ye, to see Hen Sherwood git his!"

CHAPTER XXI
IN THE TAMARACK SWAMP

The harsh tone of the unseen man terrified Nan Sherwood; but the words he spoke about her Uncle Henry inspired her to creep nearer that she might see who it was, and hear more. The fact that she was eavesdropping did not deter the girl.

She believed her uncle's life to be in peril!

The dampness between the logs of the roadway oozed up in little pools and steamed in the hot blaze of the afternoon sun. Insects buzzed and hummed, so innumerable that the chorus of their voices was like the rumble of a great church-organ.

Nan stepped from the road and pushed aside the thick underbrush to find a dry spot to place her foot. The gnats danced before her and buzzed in her ears. She brushed them aside and so pushed on until she could see the road again. A lean, yellow horse, tackled to the shafts of a broken top-buggy with bits of rope as well as worn straps, stood in the roadway. The man on the seat, talking to another on the ground, was Mr. Gedney Raffer, the timberman who was contending at law with Uncle Henry.

It was he who had said: "I'd give money, I tell ye, to see Hen Sherwood git his."

There had fallen a silence, but just as Nan recognized the mean looking old man on the carriage seat, she heard the second man speak from the other side of the buggy.

"I tell you like I done Hen himself, Ged; I don't wanter be mixed up in no land squabble. I ain't for neither side."

It was Toby. Nan knew his voice, and she remembered how he had answered Uncle Henry at the lumber camp, the first day she had seen the old lumberman. Nan could not doubt that the two men were discussing the argument over the boundary of the Perkins Tract.

Gedney Raffer snarled out an imprecation when old Toby had replied as above. "Ef you know which side of your bread the butter's on, you'll side with me," he said.

"We don't often have butter on our bread, an' I ain't goin' ter side with nobody," grumbled Toby Vanderwiller.

"S-s!" hissed Raffer. "Come here!"

Toby stepped closer to the rattletrap carriage. "You see your way to goin' inter court an' talkin' right, and you won't lose nothin' by it, Tobe."

"Huh? Only my self-respect, I s'pose," grunted the old lumberman, and Nan approved very much of him just then.

"Bah!" exclaimed Raffer.

"Bah, yourself!" Toby Vanderwiller returned with some heat. "I got some decency left, I hope. I ain't goin' to lie for you, nor no other man, Ged Raffer!"

"Say! Would it be lyin' ef you witnessed on my side?" demanded the eager Raffer.

"That's my secret," snapped the old lumberman. "If I don't witness for you, be glad I don't harm you."

"You dare!" cried Raffer, shaking his fist at the other as he leaned from the buggy seat.

"You hearn me say I wouldn't go inter court one way or 'tother," repeated Toby, gloomily.

"Wal," snarled Raffer, "see't ye don't see't ye don't. 'Specially for any man but me. Ye 'member what I told ye, Tobe. Money's tight and I oughter call in that loan."

Toby was silent for half a minute. Then Nan heard him sigh.

"Well, Ged," he observed, "it's up to you. If you take the place it'll be the poorhouse for that unforchunit boy of mine and mebbe for the ol' woman, 'specially if I can't strike a job for next winter. These here lumber bosses begin to think I'm too stiff in the j'ints."

"Wal, wal!" snarled Raffer. "I can't help it. How d'ye expec' I kin help you ef you won't help me?"

He clucked to the old horse, which awoke out of its drowse with a start, and moved on sluggishly. Toby stood in the road and watched him depart. Nan thought the old lumberman's to be the most sorrowful figure she had ever seen.

Her young heart beat hotly against the meanness and injustice of Gedney Raffer. He had practically threatened Toby with foreclosure on his little farm if the old lumberman would not help him in his contention with Mr. Sherwood. On the other hand, Uncle Henry desired his help; but Uncle Henry, Nan knew, would not try to bribe the old lumberman. Under these distressing circumstances, which antagonist's interests was Toby Vanderwiller likely to serve?

This query vastly disturbed Nan Sherwood. All along she had desired much to help Uncle Henry solve his big problem. The courts would not allow him to cut a stick of timber on the Perkins Tract until a resurvey of the line was made by government-appointed surveyors, and that would be, when?

Uncle Henry's money was tied up in the stumpage lease, or first payment to the owners of the land. It was a big contract and he had expected to pay his help and further royalties on the lease, from the sale of the timber he cut on the tract. Besides, many valuable trees had been felled before the injunction was served, and lay rotting on the ground. Every month they lay there decreased their value.

And now, it appeared, Gedney Raffer was doing all in his power to influence old Toby to serve as a witness in his, Raffer's, interests.

Had toby been willing to go into court and swear that the line of the Perkins Tract was as Mr. Sherwood claimed, the court would have to vacate the injunction and Uncle Henry could risk going ahead and cutting and hauling timber from the tract. Uncle Henry believed Toby knew exactly where the line lay, for he had been a landloper, or timber-runner in this vicinity when the original survey was made, forty-odd years before.

It was plain to Nan, hiding in the bushes and watching the old man's face, that he was dreadfully tempted. Working as hard as he might, summer and winter alike, Toby Vanderwiller had scarcely been able to support his wife and grandson. His occasional attacks of rheumatism so frequently put him back. If Raffer took away the farm and the shelter they had, what would become of them?

Uncle Henry was so short of ready money himself that he could not assume the mortgage if Raffer undertook to foreclose.

"Oh, dear me! If Momsey would only write to me that she is really rich," thought Nan, "I'd beg her for the money. I'll tell her all about poor Toby in my very next letter and maybe, if she gets all that money from the courts in Scotland, she will let me give Toby enough to pay off the mortgage."

She never for a moment doubted that Uncle Henry's contention about the timber tract line was right. He must be correct, and old Toby must know it! That is the way Nan Sherwood looked at the matter.

But now, seeing Toby turning back along the corduroy road, and slowly shuffling toward home, she stepped out of the hovering bushes and walked hastily after him. She overtook him not many yards beyond the spot where he had stood talking with Raffer. He looked startled when she spoke his name.

"Well! You air a sight for sore eyes, Sissy," he said; but added, nervously, "How in Joe Tunket did you git in the swamp? Along the road?"

"Yes, sir," said Nan.

"Come right erlong this way?"

"Yes, sir."

"Did ye meet anybody?" demanded old Toby, eyeing her sharply.

"Mr. Raffer, driving his old buckskin horse. That's all."

"Didn't say nothin' to ye, did he?" asked Toby, curiously.

"Not a word," replied Nan, honestly. "I'm afraid of him and I hid in the bushes till he had gone by."

"Huh!" sighed Toby, as though relieved. "Jest as well. Though Ged wouldn't ha' dared touch ye, Sissy."

"Never mind. I'm here now," said Nan, brightly. "And I want you to show me your house and introduce me to Mrs. Vanderwiller."

"Sure. My ol' woman will be glad to see ye," said the man, briskly. "'Tain't more'n a mile furder on."

But first they came to a deserted place, a strip more than half a mile wide, where the trees had been cut in a broad belt through the swamp. All Nan could see was sawdust and the stumps of felled trees sticking out of it. The sawdust, Toby said, was anywhere from two to twenty feet deep, and there were acres of it.

"They had their mill here, ye kin see the brick work yonder. They hauled out the lumber by teams past my place. The stea'mill was here more'n two years. They hauled the sawdust out of the way and dumped it in ev'ry holler, jest as it come handy."

"What a lot there is of it!" murmured Nan, sniffing doubtfully at the rather unpleasant odor of the sawdust.

"I wish't 'twas somewhere else," grunted Toby.

"Why-so?"

"Fire git in it and it'd burn till doomsday. Fire in sawdust is a mighty bad thing. Ye see, even the road here is made of sawdust, four foot or more deep and packed as solid as a brick walk. That's the way Pale Lick went, sawdust afire. Ha'f the town was built on sawdust foundation an' she smouldered for weeks before they knowed of it. Then come erlong a big wind and started the blaze to the surface."

"Oh!" murmured Nan, much interested. "Didn't my Uncle Henry live there then?"

"I sh'd say he did," returned Toby, emphatically. "Didn't he never tell ye about it?"

"No, sir. They never speak of Pale Lick."

"Well, I won't, nuther," grunted old Toby. "'Taint pretty for a young gal like you to hear about. Whush! Thar goes a loon!"

A big bird had suddenly come into sight, evidently from some nearby water-hole. It did not fly high and seemed very clumsy, like a duck or goose.

"Oh! Are they good to eat, Mr. Vanderwiller?" cried Nan. "Rafe brought in a brace of summer ducks the other day, and they were awfully good, the way Aunt Kate cooked them."

"Well!" drawled Toby, slyly, "I've hearn tell ye c'd eat a loon, ef 'twas cooked right. But I never tried it."

"How do you cook a loon, Mr. Vanderwiller?" asked Nan, interested in all culinary pursuits.

"Well, they tell me thet it's some slow process," said the old man, his eyes twinkling. "Ye git yer loon, pluck an' draw it, let it soak overnight in vinegar an' water, vitriol vinegar they say is the best. Then ye put it in the pot an' let it simmer all day."

"Yes?" queried the perfectly innocent Nan.

"Then ye throw off that water," Toby said, soberly, "and ye put on fresh water an' let it cook all the next day."

"Oh!"

"An' then ye throw in a piece of grin'stone with the loon, and set it to bilin' again. When ye kin stick a fork in the grin'stone, the loon's done!"

Nan joined in Toby's loud laugh at this old joke, and pretty soon thereafter they came to the hummock on which the Vanderwillers lived.

CHAPTER XXII
ON THE ISLAND

In the winter it was probably dreary enough; but now the beauty of the swelling knoll where the little whitewashed house stood, with the tiny fields that surrounded it, actually made Nan's heart swell and the tears come into her eyes.

It seemed to her as though she had never seen the grass so green as here, and the thick wood that encircled the little farm was just a hedge of blossoming shrubs with the tall trees shooting skyward in unbroken ranks. A silver spring broke ground at the corner of the paddock fence. A pool had been scooped out for the cattle to drink at; but it was not muddied, and the stream tinkled down over the polished pebbles to the wider, more sluggish stream that meandered away from the farm into the depths of the swamp.

Toby told her, before they reached the hummock, that this stream rose in the winter and flooded all about the farm, so that the latter really was an island. Unless the ice remained firm they sometimes could not drive out with either wagon or sled for days at a time.

"Then you live on an island," cried Nan.

"Huh! Ye might say so," complained Toby. "And sometimes we feel like as though we was cast away on one, too."

But the girl thought it must really be great fun to live on an island.

They went up to the house along the bank of the clear stream. On the side porch, vine-covered to the eaves, sat an old woman rocking in a low chair and another figure in what seemed at a distance, to be a child's wagon of wickerwork, but with no tongue and a high back to it.

"Here's Gran'pop!" cried a shrill voice and the little wagon moved swiftly to the edge of the steps. Nan almost screamed in fear as it pitched downward. But the wheels did not bump over the four steps leading to the ground, for a wide plank had been laid slantingly at that side, and over this the wheels ran smoothly, if rapidly.

"You have a care there, Corson!" shrilled the old lady after the cripple. "Some day you'll break your blessed neck."

Nan thought he was a little boy, until they met. Then she was surprised to see a young man's head set upon a shriveled child's body! Corson Vanderwiller had a broad brow, a head of beautiful, brown, wavy hair, and a fine mustache. He was probably all of twenty-five years old.

But Nan soon learned that the poor cripple was not grown in mind, more than in body, to that age. His voice was childish, and his speech and manner, too. He was bashful with Nan at first; then chattered like a six-year-old child to her when she had once gained his confidence.

He wheeled himself about in the little express wagon very well indeed, old Toby having rigged brakes with which he moved the wagon and steered it. His arms and hands were quite strong, and when he wished to get back on to the piazza, he seized a rope his grandfather had hung there, and dragged himself, wagon and all, up the inclined plane, or gangplank, as it might be called.

He showed Nan all his treasures, and they included some very childish toys, a number of them showing the mechanical skill of his grandfather's blunt fingers. But among them, too, were treasures from the swamp and woods that were both very wonderful and very beautiful.

Old Toby had made Corson a neatly fitted cabinet in which were specimens of preserved butterflies and moths, most of them of the gay and common varieties; but some, Nan was almost sure, were rare and valuable. There was one moth in particular, with spread wings, on the upper side of the thorax of which was traced in white the semblance of a human skull. Nan was almost sure that this must be the famous death's-head moth she had read about in school; but she was not confident enough to say anything to old Toby Vanderwiller. A few specimens of this rare insect have been found in the swamps of America, although it was originally supposed to be an Old World moth.

Nan did say, however, to Toby that perhaps some of these specimens might be bought by collectors. The pressed flowers were pretty but not particularly valuable. In the museum at the Tillbury High School there was a much finer collection from the Indiana swamps.

"Sho!" said Toby, slowly; "I wouldn't wanter sell the boy's pretties. I brung most on 'em home to him; but he mounted 'em himself."

Nan suspected that old Mrs. Vanderwiller had much to do with the neat appearance of the cabinet. She was a quiet, almost a speechless, old lady. But she was very kind and she set out her best for Nan's luncheon before the girl from Tillbury returned home.

"We ain't got much here on the island," the old lady said; "but we do love to have visitors. Don't we, Corson?"

"Nice ones," admitted the cripple, munching cake.

He had heard something of what Nan suggested to Toby about the moths and other specimens. So when the old lady was absent from the porch he whispered:

"Say, girl!"

"Well?" she asked, smiling at him.

"Is what's in that cabinet wuth as much as a dollar?"

"Oh! I expect so," said Nan. "More."

"Will you give me a dollar for 'em?" he asked, eagerly.

"Oh, I couldn't! But perhaps I can write to somebody who would be interested in buying some of your things, and for much more than a dollar."

Corson looked disappointed. Nan asked, curiously: "Why do you want the dollar?"

"To git Gran'mom a silk dress," he said promptly. "She's admired to have one all her life, and ain't never got to git it yet."

"I'm sure that's nice of you," declared Nan, warmly. "I'll try to sell some of your collection."

"Well!" he jerked out. "It's got to be pretty soon, or she won't git to wear it much. I heard her tell Gran'pop so."

This impressed Nan Sherwood as being very pitiful, for she was of a sympathetic nature. And it showed that Corson Vanderwiller, even if he was simple-minded, possessed one of the great human virtues, gratitude.

CHAPTER XXIII
A MYSTERY

On this, her first visit to the island in the swamp, Nan said nothing to old Toby Vanderwiller about the line dispute between her uncle and Gedney Raffer, which the old lumberman was supposed to be able to settle if he would.

Mrs. Vanderwiller insisted upon Toby's hitching up an old, broken-kneed pony he owned, and taking her over the corduroy road to Pine Camp, where she arrived before dark. To tell the truth, little Margaret Llewellen was not the only person who thought it odd that Nan should want to go to see the Vanderwillers in the heart of the tamarack swamp. Nan's uncle and aunt and cousins considered their guest a little odd; but they made no open comment when the girl arrived at home after her visit.

Nan was full of the wonders she had seen, commonplace enough to her relatives who had lived all their lives in touch with the beautiful and queer things of Nature as displayed in the Michigan Peninsula. Perhaps none but Tom appreciated her ecstasy over crippled Corson Vanderwiller's collection.

Rafe was inclined to poke good-natured fun at his young cousin for her enthusiasm; but Tom showed an understanding that quite surprised Nan. Despite his simplicity regarding some of the commonest things of the great outside world, he showed that he was very observant of the things about him.

"Oh, Tom was always like that," scoffed Rafe, with ready laughter at his slow brother. "He'd rather pick up a bug any day and put it through a cross-examination, than smash it under the sole of his boot."

"I don't think bugs were made to smash," Tom said stoutly.

"Whew! What in thunder were they made for?" demanded the mocking Rafe.

"I don't think God Almighty made things alive just for us to make 'em dead," said Tom, clumsily, and blushing a deep red.

Rafe laughed again. Rafe had read much more in a desultory fashion than Tom.

"Tom ought to be one of those Brahmas," he said, chuckling. "They carry a whisk broom to brush off any seat they may sit on before they sit down, so's they sha'n't crush an ant, or any other crawling thing. They're vegetarians, too, and won't take life in any form."

"Now, Rafe!" exclaimed his mother, who was never quite sure when her younger son was playing the fool. "You know that Brahmas are hens. I've got some in my flock those big white and black, lazy fowls, with feathers on their legs."

Nan had to laugh at that as well as Rafe. "Brahma fowl, I guess, came from Brahma, or maybe Brahmaputra, all right. But Rafe means Brahmans. They're a religious people of India," the girl from Tillbury said.

"And maybe they've got it right," Tom said stubbornly. "Why should we kill unnecessarily?"

Nan could have hugged him. At any rate, a new feeling for him was born at that moment, and she applauded. Aunt Kate said:

"Tom always was soft-hearted," and her big son became silent. She might as well have called him "soft-headed"; but Nan began better to appreciate Tom's worth from that time on.

Rafe remained in her eyes still the reckless, heroic figure he had seemed when running over the logs the day of the timber drive. But she began to confide in Tom after this evening of her return from the tamarack swamp.

However, this is somewhat in advance of the story. The pleasant evening passed as usual until bedtime came for Nan. She retired to her east chamber, for the windows of which Tom had made screens to keep out the night-flying insects. No matter how tired she was at night there was one thing Nan Sherwood seldom forgot.

Possibly it was silly in a girl who was almost through her freshman year at high school, but Nan brought out Beautiful Beulah and rocked her, and hugged her, and crooned over her before she went to bed. She was such a comfort!

So Nan, on this evening, went first of all to the closet and reached down to draw out the box in which she had kept the doll hidden ever since coming to Pine Camp.

It was not there!

At first Nan Sherwood could not believe this possible. She dropped on her knees and scrambled over the floor of her closet, reaching under the hanging skirts and frocks, her fear rising, second by second.

The box was not in its place. She arose and looked about her room wildly. Of course, she had not left it anywhere else, that was out of the question.

She could scarcely believe that any member of the family had been in her room, much less would disturb anything that was hers. Not even Aunt Kate came to the east chamber often. Nan had insisted upon taking care of the room, and she swept and dusted and cleaned like the smart little housewife she was. Aunt Kate had been content to let her have her way in this.

Of course Nan never locked her door. But who would touch a thing belonging to her? And her doll! Why, she was sure the family did not even know she had such a possession.

Almost wildly the girl ran out of her chamber and into the sitting room, where the family was still gathered around the evening lamp, Rafe cleaning his shot-gun, Tom reading slowly the local paper, published at the Forks, Aunt Kate mending, and Uncle Henry sitting at the open window with his pipe.

"Oh, it's gone!" gasped Nan, as she burst into the room.

"What's gone?" asked Aunt Kate, and Uncle Henry added: "What's happened to you, honey-bird?"

"My Beulah!" cried Nan, almost sobbing. "My Beulah, she's been taken!"

"My mercy, child!" cried Aunt Kate, jumping up. "Are you crazy?"

"Who's Beulah?" demanded Rafe, looking up from his gun and, Nan thought, showing less surprise than the others.

"My Beulah doll," said Nan, too troubled now to care whether the family laughed at her or not. "My Beautiful Beulah. Somebody's played a trick."

"A doll!" shouted Rafe, and burst into a chatter of laughter.

"Mercy me, child!" repeated Aunt Kate. "I didn't know you had a doll." "Got a baby rattle, too, Sissy?" chuckled Rafe. "And a ring to cut your teeth on? My, my!"

"Stop that, Rafe!" commanded his father, sternly, while Tom flushed and glared angrily at his brother.

"I didn't know you had a doll, Nannie," said Mrs. Sherwood, rather weakly. "Where'd you have it?"

"In my closet," choked Nan. "She's a great, big, beautiful thing! I know somebody must be playing a joke on me."

"Nobody here, Nannie," said Uncle Henry, with decision. "You may be sure of that." But he looked at Rafe sternly. That young man thought it the better part of wisdom to say no more.

In broken sentences the girl told her innocent secret, and why she had kept the doll hidden. Aunt Kate, after, all, seemed to understand.

"My poor dear!" she crooned, patting Nan's hand between her hard palms. "We'll all look for the dolly. Surely it can't have been taken out of the house."

"And who'd even take it out of her closet?" demanded Tom, almost as stern as his father.

"It surely didn't walk away of itself," said Aunt Kate.

She took a small hand lamp and went with Nan to the east chamber. They searched diligently, but to no good end, save to assure Nan that Beulah had utterly disappeared.

As far as could be seen the screens at the windows of the bedroom had not been disturbed. But who would come in from outside to steal Nan's doll? Indeed, who would take it out of the closet, anyway? The girl was almost sure that nobody had known she had it. It was strange, very strange indeed.

Big girl that she was, Nan cried herself to sleep that night over the mystery. The loss of Beulah seemed to snap the last bond that held her to the little cottage in Amity street, where she had spent all her happy childhood.

CHAPTER XXIV
THE SMOKING TREE

Nan awoke to a new day with the feeling that the loss of her treasured doll must have been a bad dream. But it was not. Another search of her room and the closet assured her that it was a horrid reality.

She might have lost many of her personal possessions without a pang; but not Beautiful Beulah. Nan could not tell her aunt or the rest of the family just how she felt about it. She was sure they would not understand.

The doll had reminded her continually of her home life. Although the stay of her parents in Scotland was much more extended than they or Nan had expected, the doll was a link binding the girl to her old home life which she missed so much.

Her uncle and aunt had tried to make her happy here at Pine Camp. As far as they could do so they had supplied the love and care of Momsey and Papa Sherwood. But Nan was actually ill for her old home and her old home associations.

On this morning, by herself in her bedroom, she cried bitterly before she appeared before the family.

"I have no right to make them feel miserable just because my heart, is, breaking," she sobbed aloud. "I won't let them see how bad I feel. But if I don't find Beulah, I just know I shall die!"

Could she have run to Momsey for comfort it would have helped, Oh, how much!

"I am a silly," Nan told herself at last, warmly. "But I cannot help it. Oh, dear! Where can Beulah have gone?"

She bathed her eyes well in the cold spring water brought by Tom that she always found in the jug outside her door in the morning, and removed such traces of tears as she could; and nobody noticed when she went out to breakfast that her eyelids were puffy and her nose a bit red.

The moment Rafe caught sight of her he began to squall, supposedly like an infant, crying:

"Ma-ma! Ma-ma! Tum an' take Too-tums. Waw! Waw! Waw!"

After all her hurt pride and sorrow, Nan would have called up a laugh at this. But Tom, who was drinking at the water bucket, wheeled with the full dipper and threw the contents into Rafe's face. That broke off the teasing cousin's voice for a moment; but Rafe came up, sputtering and mad.

"Say! You big oaf!" he shouted. "What you trying to do?"

"Trying to be funny," said Tom, sharply. "And you set me the example."

"Now, boys!" begged Aunt Kate. "Don't quarrel."

"And, dear me, boys," gasped Nan, "please don't squabble about me."

"That big lummox!" continued Rafe, still angry. "Because dad backs him up and says he ought to lick me, he does this. I'm going to defend myself. If he does a thing like that again, I'll fix him."

Tom laughed in his slow way and lumbered out. Uncle Henry did not hear this, and Nan was worried. She thought Aunt Kate was inclined to side with her youngest boy. Rafe would always be "the baby" to Aunt Kate.

At any rate Nan was very sorry the quarrel had arisen over her. And she was careful to say nothing to fan further the flame of anger between her cousins. Nor did she say anything more about the lost doll. So the family had no idea how heartsore and troubled the girl really was over the mystery.

It hurt her the more because she could talk to nobody about Beulah. There was not a soul in whom she could confide. Had Bess Harley been here at Pine Camp Nan felt that she could not really expect sympathy from her chum at this time; for Bess considered herself quite grown up and her own dolls were relegated to the younger members of her family.

Nan could write to her chum, however, and did. She could write to Momsey, and did that, too; not forgetting to tell her absent parents about old Toby Vanderwiller, and his wife and his grandson, and of their dilemma. If only Momsey's great fortune came true, Nan was sure that Gedney Raffer would be paid off and Toby would no longer have the threat of dispossession held over him.

Nan Sherwood wrote, too, to Mr. Mangel, the principal of the Tillbury High School, and told him about the collection the crippled grandson of the old lumberman had made, mentioning those specimens which had impressed her most. She had some hope that the strange moth might be very valuable.

Nan was so busy writing letters, and helping Aunt Kate preserve some early summer fruit, that she did not go far from the house during the next few days, and so did not see even Margaret Llewellen. The other girl friends she had made at Pine Camp lived too far away for her to visit them often or have them come to call on her.

A long letter from Papa Sherwood about this time served to take Nan's mind off the mystery, in part, at least. It was a nice letter and most joyfully received by the girl; but to her despair it gave promise of no very quick return of her parents from Scotland:

"Those relatives of your mother's whom we have met here, Mr. Andrew Blake's family, for instance, have treated us most kindly. They are, themselves, all well-to-do, and gentlefolk as well. The disposal by Old Hughie Blake, as he was known hereabout, of his estate makes no difference to the other Blakes living near Emberon," wrote Mr. Sherwood.

"It is some kin at a distance, children of a half sister of Old Hughie, who have made a claim against the estate. Mr. Andrew Blake, who is well versed in the Scotch law, assures us these distant relatives have not the shadow of a chance of winning their suit. He is so sure of this that he has kindly offered to advance certain sums to your mother to tide us over until the case is settled.

"I am sending some money to your Uncle Henry for your use, if any emergency should arise. You must not look for our return, my dear Nancy, too soon. Momsey's health is so much improved by the sea voyage and the wonderfully invigorating air here, that I should be loath to bring her home at once, even if the matter of the legacy were settled. By the way, the sum she will finally receive from Mr. Hugh Blake's estate will be quite as much as the first letter from the lawyer led us to expect. Some of your dearest wishes, my dear, may be realized in time."

"Oh! I can go to Lakeview Hall with Bess, after all!" cried Nan, aloud, at this point.

Indeed, that possibility quite filled the girl's mind for a while. Nothing else in Papa Sherwood's letter, aside from the good news of Momsey's improved health, so pleased her as this thought. She hastened to write a long letter to Bess Harley, with Lakeview Hall as the text.

Summer seemed to stride out of the forest now, full panoplied. After the frost and snow of her early days at Pine Camp, Nan had not expected such heat. The pools beside the road steamed. The forest was atune from daybreak to midnight with winged denizens, for insect and bird life seemed unquenchable in the Big Woods.

Especially was this true of the tamarack swamp. It was dreadfully hot at noontide on the corduroy road which passed Toby Vanderwiller's little farm; but often Nan Sherwood went that way in the afternoon. Mr. Mangel, the school principal, had written Nan and encouraged her to send a full description of some of Corson Vanderwiller's collection, especially of the wonderful death's-head moth, to a wealthy collector in Chicago. Nan did this at once.

So, one day, a letter came from the man and in it was a check for twenty-five dollars.

"This is a retainer," the gentleman wrote. "I am much interested in your account of the lame boy's specimens. I want the strangely marked moth in any case, and the check pays for an option on it until I can come and see his specimens personally."

Nan went that very afternoon to the tamarack swamp to tell the Vanderwillers this news and give Toby the check. She knew poor Corson would be delighted, for now he could purchase the longed-for silk dress for his grandmother.

The day was so hot and the way so long that Nan was glad to sit down when she reached the edge of the sawdust strip, to rest and cool off before attempting this unshaded desert. A cardinal bird—one of the sauciest and most brilliant of his saucy and brilliant race, flitted about her as she sat upon a log.

"You pretty thing!" crooned Nan. "If it were not wicked I'd wish to have you at home in a cage. I wish—"

She stopped, for in following the flight of the cardinal her gaze fastened upon a most surprising thing off at some distance from the sawdust road. A single dead tree, some forty feet in height and almost limbless, stood in solemn grandeur in the midst of the sawdust waste. It had been of no use to the woodcutters and they had allowed the shell of the old forest monarch to stand. Now, from its broken top, Nan espied a thin, faint column of blue haze rising.

It was the queerest thing! It was not mist, of course and she did not see how it could be smoke. There was no fire at the foot of the tree, for she could see the base of the bole plainly. She even got up and ran a little way out into the open in order to see the other side of the dead tree.

The sky was very blue, and the air was perfectly still. Almost Nan was tempted to believe that her eyes played her false. The column was almost the color of the sky itself, and it was thin as a veil.

How could there be a fire in the top of that tall tree?

"There just isn't! I don't believe I see straight!" declared Nan to herself, moving on along the roadway. "But I'll speak to Toby about it."

CHAPTER XXV
THE TEMPEST

Nan, however, did not mention to Toby the haze rising from the dead tree. In the first place, when she reached the little farm on the island in the tamarack swamp, old Toby Vanderwiller was not at home. His wife greeted the girl warmly, and Corson was glad to see her. When Nan spread the check before him and told him what it was for, and what he could do with so much money, the crippled boy was delighted.

It was a secret between them that the grandmother was to have the black silk dress that she had longed for all her married life; only Nan and Corson knew that Nan was commissioned to get the check cashed and buy the dress pattern at the Forks; or send to a catalogue house for it if she could not find a suitable piece of goods at any of the local stores.

Nan lingered, hoping that Toby would come home. It finally grew so late that she dared not wait longer. She had been warned by Aunt Kate not to remain after dusk in the swamp, nor had she any desire to do so.

Moreover there was a black cloud rolling up from the west. That was enough to make the girl hurry, for when it rained in the swamp, sometimes the corduroy road was knee deep in water.

The cloud had increased to such proportions when Nan was half way across the sawdust desert that she began to run. She had forgotten all about the smoking tree.

Not a breath of air was stirring as yet; but there was the promise of wind in that cloud. The still leaves on the bushes, the absence of bird life overhead, the lazy drone of insects, portended a swift change soon. Nan was weather-wise enough to know that.

She panted on, stumbling through the loose sawdust, but stumbling equally in the ruts; for the way was very rough. This road was lonely enough at best; but it seemed more deserted than ever now.

A red fox, his tail depressed, shot past her, and not many yards away. It startled Nan, for it seemed as though something dreadful was about to happen and the fox knew it and was running away from it.

She could not run as fast as the fox; but Nan wished that she could. And she likewise wished with all her heart that she would meet somebody.

That somebody she hoped would be Tom. Tom was drawing logs from some point near, she knew. A man down the river had bought some timber and they had been cut a few weeks before. Tom was drawing them out of the swamp for the man; and he had mentioned only that morning at breakfast that he was working within sight of the sawdust tract and the corduroy road.

Nan felt that she would be safe with big, slow Tom. Even the thought of thunder and lightning would lose some of its terrors if she could only get to Tom.

Suddenly she heard a voice shouting, then the rattle of chain harness. The voice boomed out a stave of an old hymn:

"On Jordan's stormy bank I stand, And cast a wishful eye."

"It's Tom!" gasped Nan, and ran harder.

She was almost across the open space now. The cooler depths of the forest were just ahead. Beyond, a road crossed the mainly-traveled swamp track at right angles to it, and this was the path Tom followed.

He was now coming from the river, going deeper into the swamp for another log. Nan continued to run, calling to him at the top of her voice.

She came in sight of the young timberman and his outfit. His wagon rattled so that he could not easily hear his cousin calling to him. He sat on the tongue of the wagon, and his big, slow-moving horses jogged along, rattling their chains in a jingle more noisy than harmonious.

The timber cart was a huge, lumbering affair with ordinary cartwheels in front but a huge pair behind with an extended reach between them; and to the axle of the rear pair of wheels the timber to be transported was swung off the ground and fastened with chains. Nan ran after the rumbling cart and finally Tom saw her.

"My mercy me!" gasped the boy, using one of his mother's favorite expressions. "What you doing here, Nan?"

"Chasing you, Tom," laughed the girl. "Is it going to rain?"

"I reckon. You'll get wet if it does."

"I don't care so much for that," confessed Nan. "But I am so afraid of thunder! Oh, there it comes."

The tempest muttered in the distance. Tom, who had pulled in his horses and stopped, looked worried. "I wish you weren't here, Nan," he said.

"How gallant you are, I declare, Tommy Sherwood," cried Nan, laughing again, and then shuddering as the growl of the thunder was repeated.

"Swamp's no place for a girl in a storm," muttered the boy.

"Well, I am here, Tommy; what are you going to do with me?" she asked him, saucily.

"If you're so scared by thunder you'd better begin by stopping your ears," he drawled.

Nan laughed. Slow Tom was not often good at repartee. "I'm going to stick by you till it's over, Tom," she said, hopping up behind him on the wagon-tongue.

"Cracky, Nan! You'll get soaked. It's going to just smoke in a few minutes," declared the anxious young fellow.

And that reminded Nan again of the smoking tree.

"Oh, Tom! Do you know I believe there is a tree afire over yonder," she cried, pointing.

"A tree afire?"

"Yes. I saw it smoking."

"My mercy me!" exclaimed Tom again. "What do you mean?"

Nan told him about the mystery. The fact that a column of smoke arose out of the top of the dead tree seemed to worry Tom. Nan became alarmed.

"Oh, dear, Tom! Do you really think it was afire?"

"I, don't know. If it was afire, it is afire now," he said. "Show me, Nan."

He turned the horses out of the beaten track through the brush and brambles, to the edge of the open place which had been heaped with sawdust from the steam-mill.

Just as they broke cover a vivid flash of lightning cleaved the black cloud that had almost reached the zenith by now, and the deep rumble of thunder changed to a sharp chatter; then followed a second flash and a deafening crash.

"Oh, Tom!" gasped Nan, as she clung to him.

"The flash you see'll never hit you, Nan," drawled Tom, trying to be comforting. "Remember that."

"It isn't so much the lightning I fear as it is the thunder," murmured Nan, in the intermission. "It just so-o-ounds as though the whole house was coming down."

"Ho!" cried Tom. "No house here, Nan."

"But— —-"

The thunder roared again. A light patter on the leaves and ground announced the first drops of the storm.

"Which tree was it you saw smoking?" asked the young fellow.

Nan looked around to find the tall, broken-topped tree. A murmur that had been rising in the distance suddenly grew to a sweeping roar. The trees bent before the blast. Particles of sawdust stung their faces. The horses snorted and sprang ahead. Tom had difficulty in quieting them.

Then the tempest swooped upon them in earnest.

CHAPTER XXVI
BUFFETED BY THE ELEMENTS

Nan knew she had never seen it rain so hard before. The falling water was like a drop-curtain, swept across the stage of the open tract of sawdust. In a few minutes they were saturated to the skin. Nan could not have been any wetter if she had gone in swimming.

"Oh!" she gasped into Tom's ear. "It is the deluge!"

"Never was, but one rain 't didn't clear up yet," he returned, with difficulty, for his big body was sheltering Nan in part, and he was facing the blast.

"I know. That's this one," she agreed. "But, it's awful."

"Say! Can you point out that tree that smoked?" asked Tom.

"Goodness! It can't be smoking now," gasped Nan, stifled with rain and laughter. "This storm would put out Vesuvius."

"Don't know him," retorted her cousin. "But it'd put most anybody out, I allow. Still, fire isn't so easy to quench. Where's the tree?"

"I can't see it, Tom," declared Nan, with her eyes tightly closed. She really thought he was too stubborn. Of course, if there had been any fire in that tree-top, this rain would put it out in about ten seconds. So Nan believed.

"Look again, Nan," urged her cousin. "This is no funning. If there's fire in this swamp."

"Goodness, gracious!" snapped Nan. "What a fuss-budget you are to be sure, Tom. If there was a fire, this rain would smother it. Oh! Did it ever pelt one so before?"

Fortunately the rain was warm, and she was not much discomforted by being wet. Tom still clung to the idea that she had started in his slow mind.

"Fire's no funning, I tell you," he growled. "Sometimes it smoulders for days and days, and weeks and weeks; then it bursts out like a hurricane."

"But the rain"

"This sawdust is mighty hard-packed, and feet deep," interrupted Tom. "The fire might be deep down."

"Why, Tom! How ridiculously you talk!" cried the girl. "Didn't I tell you I saw the smoke coming out of the top of a tree? Fire couldn't be deep down in the sawdust and the smoke come out of the tree top."

"Couldn't, heh?" returned Tom. "Dead tree, wasn't it?"

"Oh, yes."

"Hollow, too, of course?"

"I don't know."

"Might be hollow clear through its length," Tom explained seriously. "The butt might be all rotted out. Just a tough shell of a tree standing there, and 'twould be a fine chimney if the fire was smouldering down at its old roots."

"Oh, Tom! I never thought of such a thing," gasped Nan.

"And you don't see the tree now?"

"Let me look! Let me look!" cried Nan, conscience-stricken.

In spite of the beating rain and wind she got to her knees, still clinging to her big cousin, and then stood upon the broad tongue of the wagon. The horses stood still with their heads down, bearing the buffeting of the storm with the usual patience of dumb beasts.

A sheer wall of water seemed to separate them from every object out upon the open land. Behind them the bulk of the forest loomed as another barrier. Nan had really never believed that rain could fall so hard. It almost took her breath.

Moreover, what Tom said about the smoking tree began to trouble the girl. She thought of the fire at Pale Lick, of which she had received hints from several people. That awful conflagration, in which she believed two children belonging to her uncle and aunt had lost their lives, had started in the sawdust.

Suddenly she cried aloud and seized Tom more tightly.

"Cracky! Don't choke a fellow!" he coughed.

"Oh, Tom!"

"Well"

"I think I see it."

"The tree that smoked?" asked her cousin.

"Yes. There!"

For the moment it seemed as though the downpour lightened. Veiled by the still falling water a straight stick rose high in the air ahead of them. Tom chirruped to the horses and made them, though unwilling, go forward.

They dragged the heavy cart unevenly. Through the heavy downpour the trail was hard to follow, and once in a while a rear wheel bumped over a stump, and Nan was glad to drop down upon the tongue again, and cling more tightly than ever to her cousin's collar.

"Sure that's it?" queried Tom, craning his neck to look up into the tall, straight tree.

"I, I'm almost sure," stammered Nan.

"I, don't, see, any, smoke," drawled Tom, with his head still raised.

The rain had almost ceased, an intermission which would not be of long duration. Nan saw that her cousin's prophecy had been true; the ground actually smoked after the downpour. The sun-heated sawdust steamed furiously. They seemed to be crossing a heated cauldron. Clouds of steam rose all about the timber cart.

"Why, Tommy!" Nan choked. "It does seem as though there must be fire under this sawdust now."

Tom brought his own gaze down from the empty tree-top with a jerk. "Hoo!" he shouted, and leaned forward suddenly to flick his off horse with the whiplash. Just then the rear wheel on that side slumped down into what seemed a veritable volcano.

Flame and smoke spurted out around the broad wheel. Nan screamed. The wind suddenly swooped down upon them, and a ball of fire, flaming sawdust was shot into the air and was tossed twenty feet by a puff of wind.

"We're over an oven!" gasped Tom, and laid the whip solidly across the backs of the frightened horses.

They plunged. Another geyser of fire and smoke spurted from the hole into which the rear wheel had slumped. Again and again the big horses flung themselves into the collars in an endeavor to get the wheel out.

"Oh, Tommy!" cried Nan. "We'll be burned up!"

"No you won't," declared her cousin, leaping down. "Get off and run, Nan."

"But you—"

"Do as I say!" commanded Tom. "Run!"

"Where, where'll I run to?" gasped the girl, leaping off the tongue, too, and away from the horses' heels.

"To the road. Get toward home!" cried Tom, running around to the rear of the timber cart.

"And leave you here?" cried Nan. "I guess not, Mr. Tom!" she murmured.

But he did not hear that. He had seized his axe and was striding toward the edge of the forest. For a moment Nan feared that Tom was running away as he advised her to do. But that would not be like Tom Sherwood!

At the edge of the forest he laid the axe to the root of a sapling about four inches through at the butt. Three strokes, and the tree was down. In a minute he had lopped off the branches for twenty feet, then removed the top with a single blow.

As he turned, dragging the pole with him, up sprang the fire again from the hollow into which the wheel of the wagon had sunk. It was a smoking furnace down there, and soon the felloe and spokes would be injured by the flames and heat. Sparks flew on the wings of the wind from out of the mouth of the hole. Some of them scattered about the horses and they plunged again, squealing.

It seemed to Nan impossible after the recent cloudburst that the fire could find anything to feed upon. But underneath the packed surface of the sawdust, the heat of summer had been drying out the moisture for weeks. And the fire had been smouldering for a long time. Perhaps for yards and yards around, the interior of the sawdust heap was a glowing furnace.

Nan would not run away and Tom did not see her. As he came plunging back to the stalled wagon, suddenly his foot slumped into the yielding sawdust and he fell upon his face. He cried out with surprise or pain. Nan, horrified, saw the flames and smoke shooting out of the hole into which her cousin had stepped. For the moment the girl felt as if her heart had stopped beating.

"Oh, Tom! Oh, Tom!" she shrieked, and sprang toward him.

Tom was struggling to get up. His right leg had gone into the yielding mass up to his hip, and despite his struggles he could not get it out. A long yellow flame shot out of the hole and almost licked his face. It, indeed, scorched his hair on one side of his head.

But Nan did not scream again. She needed her breath, all that she could get, for a more practical purpose. Her cousin waved her back feebly, and tried to tell her to avoid the fire.

Nan rushed in, got behind him, and seized her cousin under the arms. To lift him seemed a giant's task; but nevertheless she tried.

CHAPTER XXVII
OLD TOBY IN TROUBLE

The squealing and plunging of the horses, the rattling of their chains, the shrieking of the wind, the reverberating cracks of thunder made a deafening chorus in Nan's ears. She could scarcely hear what the imperiled Tom shouted to her. Finally she got it:

"Not that way! Pull sideways!"

He beat his hands impotently upon the crust of sawdust to the left. Nan tugged that way. Tom pulled, too, heaving his great body upward, and scratching and scrambling along the sawdust with fingers spread like claws. His right leg came out of the hole, and just then the rain descended torrentially again.

The flames from this opening in the roof of the furnace were beaten down. Tom got to his feet, shaking and panting. He hobbled painfully when he walked.

But in a moment he seized upon the pole he had dropped and made for the smoking timber cart. The terrified horses tried again and again to break away; but the chain harnesses were too strong; nor did the mired wheel budge.

"Oh, Tom! Oh, Tom!" begged Nan. "Let us make the poor horses free, and run ourselves."

"And lose my wagon?" returned her cousin, grimly. "Not much!"

The rain, which continued to descend with tropical violence, almost beat Nan to the ground; but Tom Sherwood worked furiously.

He placed the butt of the lever he had cut under the hub of the great wheel. There was a sound stump at hand to use as a fulcrum. Tom threw himself upon the end of the lever. Nan ran to add her small weight to the endeavor. The wheel creaked and began to rise slowly.

The sawdust was not clinging, it was not like real mire. There was no suction to hold the wheel down. Merely the crust had broken in and the wheel had encountered an impediment of a sound tree root in front of it so that, when the horses tugged, the tire had come against the root and dragged back the team.

Out poured the flames and smoke again, the flames hissing as they were quenched by the falling water. Higher, higher rose the cart wheel. Nan, who was behind her cousin, saw his neck and ears turn almost purple from the strain he put in the effort to dislodge the wheel. Up, up it came, and then——-

"Gid-ap! 'Ap, boys! Yah! Gid-ap!"

The horses strained. The yoke chains rattled. Tom gasped to Nan:

"Take my whip! Quick! Let 'em have it!"

The girl had always thought the drover's whip Tom used a very cruel implement, and she wished he did not use it. But she knew now that it was necessary. She leaped for the whip which Tom had thrown down and showed that she knew its use.

The lash hissed and cracked over the horses' backs. Tom voiced one last, ringing shout. The cart wheel rose up, the horses leaped forward, and the big timber cart was out of its plight.

Flames and smoke poured out of the hole again. The rain dashing upon and into the aperture could not entirely quell the stronger element. But the wagon was safe, and so, too, were the two cousins.

Tom was rather painfully burned and Nan began to cry about it. "Oh! Oh! You poor, poor dear!" she sobbed. "It must smart you dreadfully, Tommy."

"Don't worry about me," he answered. "Get aboard. Let's get out of this."

"Are you going home?"

"Bet you!" declared Tom. "Why, after this rain stops, this whole blamed place may be in flames. Must warn folks and get out the fire guard."

"But the rain will put out the fire, Tom," said Nan, who could not understand even now the fierce power of a conflagration of this kind.

"Look there!" yelled Tom, suddenly glancing back over her head as she sat behind him on the wagon tongue.

With a roar like an exploding boiler, the flames leaped up the heart of the hollow tree. The bursted crust of the sawdust heap had given free ingress to the wind, and a draught being started, it sucked the flames directly up the tall chimney the tree made.

The fire burst from the broken top. The flames met the falling rain as though they were unquenchable. Indeed the clouds were scattering, and second by second the downfall was decreasing. The tempest of rain was almost over; but the wind remained to fan the flames that had now broken cover in several spots, as well as through the tall and hollow tree.

Tom hastened his team toward the main road that passed through the tamarack swamp. At one end of it was Pine Camp; in the other direction, after passing the knoll on which the Vanderwillers lived, the roadway came out upon a more traveled road to the forks and the railroad.

Pine Camp was the nearest place where help could be secured to beat down the fire, if, indeed, this were at all possible. There was a telephone line there which, in a roundabout way, could be made to carry the news of the forest fire to all the settlements in the Big Woods and along the railroad line.

But Nan seized Tom's arm and shook it to call his attention as the horses neared the road.

"Tom! For goodness' sake!" she gasped.

"What's the matter now?" her cousin demanded, rather sharply, for his burns were painful.

"Toby, the Vanderwillers! What will become of them?"

"What d'you mean?" asked Tom, aghast.

"That poor cripple! They can't get away, he and his grandmother. Perhaps Toby hasn't come home yet."

"And the wind's that way," Tom interrupted.

It was indeed. The storm had come up from the west and the wind was still blowing almost directly into the east. A sheet of flame flew from the top of the old dead tree even as the boy spoke, and was carried toward the thick forest. It did not reach it, and as the blazing brand fell it was quenched on the wet surface of the sawdust.

Nevertheless, the fire was spreading under the crust and soon the few other dead trees left standing on the tract would burst into flame. As they looked, the fire burst out at the foot of the tree and began to send long tongues of flame licking up the shredded bark.

The effect of the drenching rain would soon be gone and the fire would secure great headway.

"Those poor folks are right in the track of the fire, I allow," admitted Tom. "I wonder if he's got a good wide fire strip ploughed?"

"Oh! I know what you mean," Nan cried. "You mean all around the edge of his farm where it meets the woods?"

"Yes. A ploughed strip may save his buildings. Fire can't easily cross ploughed ground. Only, if these woods get really ablaze, the fire will jump half a mile!"

"Oh no, Tom! You don't mean that?"

"Yes, I do," said her cousin, gloomily. "Tobe's in a bad place. You don't know what a forest fire means, nor the damage it does, Nannie. I'm right troubled by old Tobe's case."

"But there's no danger for Pine Camp, is there?" asked the girl, eagerly.

"Plenty of folks there to make a fire-guard. Besides, the wind's not that way, exactly opposite. And she's not likely to switch around so soon, neither. I, don't, know"

"The folks at home ought to know about it," Nan interrupted.

"They'll know it, come dark," Tom said briefly. "They'll be looking for you and they'll see the blaze. Why! After dark that old dead tree will look like a lighthouse for miles 'n' miles!"

"I suppose it will," agreed Nan. "But I do want to get home, Tom."

"Maybe the storm's not over," said her cousin, cocking an eye towards the clouded heavens. "If it sets in for a long rain (and one's due about this time according to the Farmer's Almanac) it would keep the fire down, put it out entirely, maybe. But we can't tell."

Nan sighed and patted his shoulder. "I know it's our duty to go to the island, Tommy. You're a conscientious old thing. Drive on."

Tom clucked to the horses. He steered them into the roadway, but headed away from home. Another boy with the pain he was bearing would not have thought of the old lumberman and his family. They were the only people likely to be in immediate danger from the fire if it spread. The cousins might easily reach the Vanderwiller's island, warn them of the fire, and return to town before it got very late, or before the fire crossed the wood-road.

They rumbled along, soon striking the corduroy road, having the thick forest on either hand again. The ditches were running bank full. Over a quagmire the logs, held down by cross timbers spiked to the sleepers, shook under the wheels, and the water spurted up through the interstices as the horses put down their heavy feet.

"An awful lot of water fell," Tom said soberly.

"Goodness! The swamp is full," agreed Nan.

"We may have some trouble in reaching Toby's place," the boy added. "But maybe—"

He halted in his speech, and the next instant pulled the horses down to a willing stop. "Hark-a-that!" whispered Tom.

"Can it be anybody crying? Maybe it's a wildcat," said Nan, with a vivid remembrance of her adventure in the snow that she had never yet told to any member of the family.

"It's somebody shouting, all right," observed Tom. "Up ahead a way. Gid-ap!"

He hurried the horses on, and they slopped through the water which, in places, flowed over the road, while in others it actually lifted the logs from their foundation and threatened to spoil the roadway entirely.

Again and again they heard the faint cry, a man's voice. Tom stood up and sent a loud cry across the swamp in answer:

"We're coming! Hold on!

"Don't know what's the matter with him," he remarked, dropping down beside Nan again, and stirring the horses to a faster pace. "S'pose he's got into a mud-hold, team and all, maybe."

"Oh, Tom! Maybe he'll be sucked right down into this awful mud."

"Not likely. There aren't many quicksands, or the like, hereabout. Never heard tell of 'em, if there are. Old Tobe lost a cow once in some slough."

They came to a small opening in the forest just then. Here a great tree had been uprooted by the wind and leaned precariously over a quagmire beside the roadway. Fortunately only some of the lower branches touched the road line and Tom could get his team around them.

Then the person in trouble came into sight. Nan and her cousin saw him immediately. He was in the middle of the shaking morass waist deep in the mire, and clinging to one of the small hanging limbs of the uprooted tree.

"Hickory splits!" ejaculated Tom, stopping the team. "It's old Tobe himself! Did you ever see the like!"

CHAPTER XXVIII
THE GIRL IN THE HOLLOW TREE

Just why old Toby Vanderwiller was clinging to that branch and did not try to wade ashore, neither Nan nor Tom could understand. But one thing was plain: the old lumberman thought himself in danger, and every once in a while he gave out a shout for help. But his voice was growing weak.

"Hey, Tobe!" yelled Tom. "Why don't you wade ashore?"

"There ye be, at last, hey?" snarled the old man, who was evidently just as angry as he could be. "Thought ye'd never come. Hearn them horses rattling their chains, must ha' been for an hour."

"That's stretching it some," laughed Tom. "That tree hasn't been toppled over an hour."

"Huh! Ye can't tell me nothin' 'beout that!" declared Toby. "I was right here when it happened."

"Goodness!" gasped Nan.

"Yep. And lemme tell ye, I only jest 'scaped being knocked down when she fell."

"My!" murmured Nan again.

"That's how I got inter this muck hole," growled the old lumberman. "I jumped ter dodge the tree, and landed here."

"Why don't you wade ashore?" demanded Tom again, preparing in a leisurely manner to cast the old man the end of a line he had coiled on the timber cart.

"Yah!" snarled Toby. "Why don't Miz' Smith keep pigs? Don't ax fool questions, Tommy, but gimme holt on that rope. I'm afraid ter let go the branch, for I'll sink, and if I try ter pull myself up by it, the whole blamed tree'll come down onter me. Ye see how it's toppling?"

It was true that the fallen tree was in a very precarious position. When Toby stirred at all, the small weight he rested on the branch made the head of the tree dip perilously. And if it did fall the old man would be thrust into the quagmire by the weight of the branches which overhung his body.

"Let go of it, Toby!" called Tom, accelerating his motions. "Catch this!"

He flung the coil with skill and Toby seized it. The rocking tree groaned and slipped forward a little. Toby gave a yell that could have been heard much farther than his previous cries.

But Tom sank back on the taut rope and fairly jerked the old man out of the miry hole. Scrambling on hands and knees, Toby reached firmer ground, and then the road itself.

Nan uttered a startled exclamation and cowered behind the cart. The huge tree, groaning and its roots splintering, sagged down and, in an instant, the spot there the old lumberman had been, was completely covered by the interlacing branches of the uprooted tree.

"Close squeal, that," remarked Tom, helping the old man to his feet.

Toby stared at them both, wiping the mire from his face as he did so. He was certainly a scarecrow figure after his submersion in the mud; gut Nan did not feel like laughing at him. The escape had been too narrow.

"Guess the Almighty sent you just in time, Tom, my boy," said Toby Vanderwiller. "He must have suthin' more for the old man to do yet, before he cashes in. And little Sissy, too. Har! Henry Sherwood's son and Henry Sherwood's niece. Reckon I owe him a good turn," he muttered.

Nan heard this, though Tom did not, and her heart leaped. She hoped that Toby would feel sufficient gratitude to help Uncle Henry win his case against Gedney Raffer. But, of course, this was not the time to speak of it.

When the old lumberman heard about the fire in the sawdust he was quite as excited as the young folk had been. It was fast growing dark now, but it was impossible from the narrow road to see even the glow of the fire against the clouded sky.

"I believe it's goin' to open up and rain ag'in," Toby said. "But if you want to go on and plow me a fire-strip, Tommy, I'll be a thousand times obleeged to you."

"That's what I came this way for," said the young fellow briefly. "Hop on and we'll go to the island as quickly as possible."

They found Mrs. Vanderwiller and the crippled boy anxiously watching the flames in the tree top from the porch of the little house on the island. Nan ran to them to relate their adventures, while Toby got out the plow and Tom hitched his big horses to it.

The farm was not fenced, for the road and forest bounded it completely. Tom put the plow in at the edge of the wood and turned his furrows toward it, urging the horses into a trot. It was not that the fire was near; but the hour was growing late and Tom knew that his mother and father would be vastly anxious about Nan.

The young fellow made twelve laps, turning twelve broad furrows that surely would guard the farm against any ordinary fire. But by the time he was done it did not look as though the fire in the sawdust would spread far. The clouds were closing up once more and it was again raining, gently but with an insistence that promised a night of downpour, at least.

Old Mrs. Vanderwiller had made supper, and insisted upon their eating before starting for Pine Camp. And Tom, at least, did his share with knife and fork, while his horses ate their measure of corn in the paddock. It was dark as pitch when they started for home, but Tom was cheerful and sure of his way, so Nan was ashamed to admit that she was frightened.

"Tell yer dad I'll be over ter Pine Camp ter see him 'fore many days," Old Toby jerked out, as they were starting. "I got suthin' to say to him, I have!"

Tom did not pay much attention to this; but Nan did. Her heart leaped for joy. She believed that Toby Vanderwiller's words promised help for Uncle Henry.

But she said nothing to Tom about it. She only clung to his shoulder as the heavy timber cart rattled away from the island.

A misty glow hung over the sawdust strip as they advanced; but now that the wind had died down the fire could not spread. Beside the road the glow worms did their feeble best to light the way; and now and then an old stump in the swamp displayed a ghostly gleam of phosphorus.

Nan had never been in the swamp before at night. The rain had driven most of the frogs and other croaking creatures to cover. But now and then a sudden rumble "Better-go-roun'!" or "Knee-deep! Knee-deep!" proclaimed the presence of the green-jacketed gentlemen with the yellow vests.

"Goodness me! I'd be scared to death to travel this road by myself," Nan said, as they rode on. "The frogs make such awful noises."

"But frogs won't hurt you," drawled Tom.

"I know all that," sighed Nan. "But they sound as if they would. There! That one says, just as plain as plain can be, 'Throw 'im in! Throw 'im in!"

"Good!" chuckled Tom. "And there's a drunken old rascal calling: 'Jug-er-rum! Jug-er-rum!'!"

A nighthawk, wheeling overhead through the rain, sent down her discordant cry. Deep in a thicket a whip-poor-will complained. It was indeed a ghostly chorus that attended their slow progress through the swamp at Pine Camp.

When they crossed the sawdust tract there was little sign of the fire. The dead tree had fallen and was just a glowing pile of coals, fast being quenched by the gently falling rain. For the time, at least, the danger of a great conflagration was past.

"Oh! I am so glad," announced Nan, impetuously. "I was afraid it was going to be like that Pale Lick fire."

"What Pale Lick fire?" demanded Tom, quickly. "What do you know about that?"

"Not much, I guess," admitted his cousin, slowly. "But you used to live there, didn't you?"

"Rafe and I don't remember anything about it," said Tom, in his quiet way. "Rafe was a baby and I wasn't much better. Marm saved us both, so we've been told. She and dad never speak about it."

"Oh! And Indian Pete?" whispered Nan.

"He saved the whole of us—dad and all. He knew a way out through a slough and across a lake. He had a dug-out. He got badly burned dragging dad to the boat when he was almost suffocated with smoke," Tom said soberly.

"'Tisn't anything we talk about much, Nan. Who told you?"

"Oh, it's been hinted to me by various people," said Nan, slowly. "But I saw Injun Pete, Tom."

"When? He hasn't been to Pine Camp since you came."

Nan told her cousin of her adventure in the hollow near Blackton's lumber camp. Tom was much excited by that.

"Gracious me, Nan! But you are a plucky girl. Wait till Rafe hears about it. And marm and dad will praise you for being so level-headed today. Aren't many girls like you, Nan, I bet!"

"Nor boys like you, Tom," returned the girl, shyly. "How brave you were, staying to pull that old wagon-wheel out of the fire."

"Ugh!" growled Tom. "A fat time I'd have had there if it hadn't been for you helping me out of the oven. Cracky! I thought I was going to have my leg burned to a cinder.

"That would have been terrible!" shuddered Nan. "What would poor Aunt Kate have said?"

"We can't tell her anything about it," Tom hastened to say. "You see, my two older brothers, Jimmy and Alfred, were asleep in the garret of our house at Pale Lick, and marm thought they'd got out. It wasn't until afterward that she learned they'd been burned up with the house. She's never got over it."

"I shouldn't think she would," sighed Nan.

"And you see she's awfully afraid of fire, even now," said Tom.

They rattled on over the logs of the road; here and there they came to bad places, where the water had not gone down; and the horses were very careful in putting their hoofs down upon the shaking logs. However, it was not much over an hour after leaving the island that they spied the lights of Pine Camp from the top of the easy rise leading out of the tamarack swamp.

They met Rafe with a lantern half way down the hill. Uncle Henry was away and Aunt Kate had sent Rafe out to look for Nan, although she supposed that the girl had remained at the Vanderwillers' until the rain was over, and that Toby would bring her home.

There was but one other incident of note before the three of them reached the rambling house Uncle Henry had built on the outskirts of Pine Camp. As they turned off the swamp road through the lane that ran past the Llewellen cottage, Rafe suddenly threw the ray of his lantern into a hollow tree beside the roadway. A small figure was there, and it darted back out of sight.

"There!" shouted Rafe. "I knew you were there, you little nuisance. What did you run out of the house and follow me for, Mar'gret Llewellen?"

He jumped in and seized the child, dragging her forth from the hollow of the big tree. He held her, while she squirmed and screamed.

"You lemme alone, Rafe Sherwood! Lemme alone!" she commanded. "I ain't doin' nothin' to you."

"Well, I bet you are up to some monkey-shines, out this time of night," said Rafe, giving her a little shake. "You come on back home, Mag."

"I won't!" declared the girl.

"Yes, do, Margaret," begged Nan. "It's going to rain harder. Don't hurt her, Rafe."

"Yah! You couldn't hurt her," said Rafe. "She's as tough as a little pine-knot, and don't you forget it! Aren't you, Mag?"

"Lemme go!" repeated Margaret, angrily.

"What did you chase down here after me for?" asked Rafe, the curious.

"I, I thought mebbe you was comin' to hunt for something," stammered the girl.

"So I was. For Nancy here," laughed Rafe.

"Thought 'twas somethin' of mine," said the girl. "Lemme go now!"

She jerked away her hand and scuttled into the house that they were then just passing.

"Wonder what the little imp came out to watch me for?" queried Rafe.

After they had arrived at home and the excitement o the return was over; after she and Tom had told as much of their adventures as they thought wise, and Nan had retired to the east chamber, she thought again about Margaret and her queer actions by the roadside.

"Why, that tree is where Margaret hides her most precious possessions," said Nan, suddenly, sitting up in bed. "Why, what could it be she was afraid Rafe would find there? Why can that child have hidden something there that she doesn't want any of us to see?"

Late as it was, and dark as it was, and stormy as the night was, she felt that she must know immediately what Margaret Llewellen had hidden in the hollow tree.

CHAPTER XXIX
GREAT NEWS FROM SCOTLAND

Nan put two and two together, and the answer came right

She got out of bed, lit her lamp again and began to dress. She turned her light down to a dim glimmer, however, for she did not want her aunt to look out of the window of her bedroom on the other side of the parlor and catch a glimpse of her light.

In the half darkness Nan made a quick toilet; and then, with her raincoat on and hood over her head, she hesitated with her hand upon the knob of the door.

"If I go through the parlor and out the side door, Aunt Kate will hear me," thought Nan. "That won't do at all."

She looked at the further window. Outside the rain was pattering and there was absolutely no light. In the pocket of her raincoat Nan had slipped the electric torch she had brought from home, something of which Aunt Kate cordially approved, and was always begging Uncle Henry to buy one like it.

The pocket lamp showed her the fastenings of the screen. Tom had made it to slide up out of the way when she wanted to open or close the sash. And, as far as she could see, any one could open it from the outside as easily as from the room itself.

"And that's just what she did," decided Nan. "How foolish of me not to think of it before."

With this enigmatical observation Nan prepared to leave the room by this very means. She was agile, and the sill of the window was only three feet from the ground. It was through this opening that she had helped Margaret Llewellen into her room on the first occasion that odd child had visited her.

Nan jumped out, let the screen down softly, and hurried across the unfenced yard to the road. She knew well enough when she reached the public track, despite the darkness for the mirey clay stuck to her shoes and made the walking difficult.

She flashed her lamp once, to get her bearings, and then set off down the lane toward the swamp road. There was not a light in any house she passed, not even in Mr. Fen Llewellen's cottage. "I guess Margaret's fast asleep," murmured Nan, as she passed swiftly on.

The rain beat down upon the girl steadily, and Nan found it shivery out here in the dark and storm. However, her reason for coming, Nan conceived, was a very serious one. This was no foolish escapade.

By showing her light now and then she managed to follow the dark lane without stepping off into any of the deep puddles which lay beside the path. She came, finally, to the spot where Rafe had met her and Tom with his lantern that evening. Here stood the great tree with a big hollow in it, Margaret Llewellen's favorite playhouse.

For a moment Nan hesitated. The place looked so dark and there might be something alive in the hollow.

But she plucked up courage and flashed her lamp into it. The white ray played about the floor of the hollow. The other Llewellen children dared not come here, for Margaret punished them if they disturbed anything belonging to her.

What Nan was looking for was not in sight. She stepped inside, and raised the torch. The rotting wood had been neatly scooped out, and where the aperture grew smaller at the top a wide shelf had been made by the ingenious Margaret. Nan had never been in this hide-out before.

"It must be here! It must be here!" she kept telling herself, and stood on her tiptoes to feel along the shelf, which was above her head.

Nan discovered nothing at first. She felt along the entire length of the shelf again. Nothing!

"I know better!" she almost sobbed. "My dear, beautiful."

She jumped up, feeling back on the shelf with her right hand. Her fingers touched something, and it was not the rotting wood of the tree!

"It's there!" breathed the excited girl. She flashed her lamp around, searching for something to stand upon. There in the corner was a roughly made footstool.

In a moment Nan had the footstool set in position, and had stepped upon it. Her hand darted to the back of the shelf. There was a long box, a pasteboard box.

Nan dropped her lamp with a little scream of ecstasy, and of course the light went out. But she had the long box clasped in her arms. She could not wait to get home with it, but tumbled off the stool and sat down upon it, picked up the torch, held it so the round spot-light gave her illumination, and untied the string.

Off came the cover. She peeped within. The pink and white loveliness of Beulah's wax features peered up at her.

In fifteen minutes Nan was back in her room, without being discovered by anybody, and with the doll safely clasped in her arms. Indeed, she went to bed a second time that night with her beloved playmate lying on the pillow beside her, just as she had done when a little girl.

"I suppose I'm foolish," she confessed to Aunt Kate the next morning when she told her about it. "But I loved Beulah so much when I was little that I can't forget her now. If I go to Lakeview Hall I'm going to take her with me. I don't care what the other girls say!"

"You are faithful in your likes, child," said Aunt Kate nodding. "'Tis a good trait. But I'd like to lay that Marg'ret Llewellen across my knee, for her capers."

"And I didn't think she cared for dolls," murmured Nan.

But it was young Bob who betrayed the mysterious reason for his sister's act.

"Huh!" he said, with a boy's disgust for such things. "Mag's crazy about pretty faces, if they're smooth, an' pink. She peeked into that Sherwood gal's room and seed her playin' doll; then she had ter have it for herself 'cause it was so pretty and had a smooth face, not like the kids' dolls that Aunt Matildy buyed."

Poor little Margaret was greatly chagrined at the discovery of her secret. She ran away into the woods whenever she saw Nan coming, for a long time thereafter. It took weeks for the girl from Tillbury to regain the half-wild girl's confidence again.

Nan was just as busy and happy as she could be, considering the uncertain news from Scotland and Uncle Henry's unfortunate affair with Gedney Raffer. She helped Aunt Kate with the housework early every morning so that they might both hurry into the woods to pick berries.

Pine Camp was in the midst of a vast huckleberry country, and at the Forks a cannery had been established. Beside, the Forks was a big shipping centre for the fresh berries.

Uncle Henry bought crates and berry "cups," and sometimes the whole family picked all day long in the berry pasture, taking with them a cold luncheon, and eating it picnic fashion.

It was great fun, Nan thought, despite the fact that she often came home so wearied that her only desire was to drop into bed. But the best part of it, the saving grace of all this toil, was the fact that she was earning money for herself! Account was faithfully kept of every cup of berries she picked, and, when Uncle Henry received his check from the produce merchant to whom he shipped the berries, Nan was paid her share.

These welcome earnings she saved for a particular purpose, and for no selfish one, you may be sure. Little Margaret Llewellen still ran from her and Nan wished to win the child back; so she schemed to do this.

After all, there was something rather pitiful in the nature of the child who so disliked any face that was "wizzled," but loved those faces that were fair and smooth.

Margaret only possessed a feeling that is quite common to humanity; she being such a little savage, she openly expressed an emotion that many of us have, but try to hide.

The Llewellen children picked berries, of course, as did most of the other neighbors. Pine Camp was almost a "deserted village" during the season when the sweet, blue fruit hung heavy on the bushes.

Sometimes the Sherwood party, and the Llewellens, would cross each others' paths in the woods, or pastures; but little Margaret always shrank into the background. If Nan tried to surprise her, the half wild little thing would slip away into the deeper woods like one of its own denizens.

Near the river one day Margaret had an experience that should have taught her a lesson, however, regarding wandering alone in the forest. And the adventure should, too, have taught the child not to shrink so from an ugly face.

Nan had something very important to tell Margaret. Her savings had amounted to quite a goodly sum and in the catalog of a mail-order house she had found something of which she wished to secure Margaret's opinion. The child, as usual, ran away when they met, and even Bob could not bring her back.

"She's as obstinate as dad's old mu-el," grunted the disgusted boy. "Can't do a thing with her, Nan Sherwood." "I'll just get her myself!" declared Nan, laughing, and she started into the thicker woods to circumvent Margaret. She did not follow the river as the smaller girl had, but struck into the bush, intending to circle around and head Margaret off.

She had not pushed her way through the clinging vines and brush for ten minutes before she heard somebody else in the jungle. She thought it was the little girl, at first; then she caught sight of a man's hat and knew that Margaret did not wear a hat at all.

"Goodness! Who can that be?" thought Nan. She was a little nervous about approaching strange people in the wood; although at this season there was nothing to apprehend from stragglers, there were so many berry pickers within call.

Nan did not seek to overtake the man, however, and would have kept on in her original direction, had she not heard a cry and a splitting crash toward the river bank. Some accident had happened, and when Nan heard the scream repeated, she was sure that the voice was that of Margaret.

So she set off directly, on a run, tearing her dress and scratching her hands and face, but paying no attention to either misfortune. She only wanted to get to the scene of the accident and lend her aid, if it was needed.

And it would have been needed if it had not been for the man whose hat she had seen a few moments before. He made his passage through the bush much quicker than could Nan, and when the latter reached an opening where she could see the river, the stranger was just leaping into the deep pool under the high bank.

It was plain to be seen what had happened. A sycamore overhung the river and somebody had climbed out upon a small branch to reach a few half-ripened grapes growing on a vine that ran up the tree.

The branch had split, drooping downward, and the adventurous grape-gatherer had been cast into the water.

"Oh, Margaret!" screamed Nan, confident that it was the reckless child that was in peril.

She hurried to the brink of the low bluff, from which the rescuer had plunged. He had already seized the child (there was an eddy here under the bank) and was striking out for the shore. Nan saw his wet face, with the bedraggled hair clinging about it.

It was the awfully scarred face of Injun Pete; but to the excited Nan, at that moment, it seemed one of the most beautiful faces she had ever seen!

The Indian reached the bank, clung to a tough root, and lifted up the gasping Margaret for Nan to reach. The girl took the child and scrambled up the bank again; by the time she was at the top, Injun Pete was beside her.

"She not hurt, Little missy," said the man, in his soft voice, and turning his face so that Nan should not see it. "She just scared."

Margaret would not even cry. She was too plucky for that. When she got her breath she croaked:

"Put me down, Nan Sherwood. I ain't no baby."

"But you're a very wet child," said Nan, laughing, yet on the verge of tears herself. "You might have been drowned, you WOULD have been had it not been for Mr. Indian Pete."

"Ugh!" whispered Margaret. "I seen him when I come up out o' that nasty water. I wanted to go down again."

"Hush, Margaret!" cried Nan, sternly. "You must thank him."

The man was just then moving away. He shook himself like a dog coming out of the stream, and paid no further attention to his own wet condition.

"Wait, please!" Nan called after him.

"She all right now," said the Indian.

"But Margaret wants to thank you, don't you, Margaret?"

"Much obleeged," said the little girl, bashfully. "You air all right, you air."

"That all right, that all right," said the man, hurriedly. "No need to thank me."

"Yes, there is," said Nan, insistently. "Come here, please. Margaret wants to kiss you for saving her life."

"Oh!" The word came out of Margaret's lips like an explosion. Nan stared very sternly at her. "If you don't," she said in a low tone, "I'll tell your father all about how you came to fall into the river."

Under this threat Margaret became amenable. She puckered up her lips and stretched her arms out toward Indian Pete. The man stumbled back and fell on his knees beside the two girls. Nan heard the hoarse sob in his throat as he took little Margaret in his arms.

"Bless you! Bless you!" he murmured, receiving the kiss right upon his scarred cheek. But Nan saw that Margaret's eyes were tightly closed as she delivered the caress, per order!

The next moment the man with the scarred face had slipped away and disappeared in the forest. They saw him no more.

However, just as soon as the catalog house could send it, Margaret received a beautiful, pink-cheeked, and flaxen-haired Doll, not as fine as Beulah, but beautiful enough to delight any reasonable child.

Nan had won back Margaret's confidence and affection.

Meanwhile the hot summer was fast passing. Nan heard from her chum, Bess Harley, with commendable regularity; and no time did Bess write without many references to Lakeview Hall.

Nan, advised by her former teacher in Tillbury, had brought her books to Pine Camp, and had studied faithfully along the lines of the high school work. She was sure she could pass quite as good an entrance examination for Lakeview Hall as Bess could.

And at last good news came from Scotland:

"I am not quite ready to bring Momsey home," Papa Sherwood wrote. "But the matter of her fortune is at least partially settled. The claims of the other relatives have been disallowed. Mr. Andrew Blake is prepared to turn over to your Momsey a part of her wonderful fortune. The rest will come later. She will tell you all about it herself.

"What I wish to say to you particularly in this letter," pursued Mr. Sherwood, "is, that arrangements have been made for you to attend Lakeview Hall this coming semester. You will meet your friend, Elizabeth Harley, in Chicago, and will go with her to the school. I am writing by this mail to the principal of the Hall. Mr. Harley has made all other necessary arrangements for you."

"Oh!" cried Nan, clasping her hands. "It's too good to be true! It can't be possible! I just know I'll wake up in a minute and find all this an exciting dream, and that's all!"

But Nan was wrong on that point, as the reader will see if her further adventures are followed in the next volume of the series, entitled, "Nan Sherwood at Lakeview Hall, or, The Mystery of the Haunted Boathouse."

While Nan was still intensely excited over this letter from Scotland, Toby Vanderwiller drove up to the Sherwood house behind his broken-kneed pony. This was the first time any of the Sherwoods had seen him since the day of the big storm and the fire in the sawdust.

CHAPTER XXX
OFF FOR LAKEVIEW HALL

Nan ran out immediately to speak to the old lumberman; but Toby was calling for Uncle Henry:

"Hey, Hen! Hen Sherwood! Come out yere," he cried.

Uncle Henry halloaed from the stables, and came striding at the call. Nan reached the old rattletrap wagon first.

"Oh, Mr. Vanderwiller!" she said. "I am glad to see you! And how is your wife and Corson?"

He looked down at her reflectively, and for a moment did not say a word. Then he swallowed something and said, jerkily:

"An' you're the one that done it all, Sissy! The ol' woman an' the boy air as chipper as bluejays. An' they air a honin' for a sight on you."

"Yes. I haven't been over lately. But that man from Chicago came, didn't he?"

"I sh'd say 'yes'! He come," said Toby, in awe. "An' what d'ye s'pose? He done buyed a heap of Corson's spec'mens an' paid him more'n a hundred dollars for 'em. And that ain't countin' that there dead-head butterfly ye made sech a time about.

"I reckoned," pursued Toby, "that you was right crazy about that there bug. One bug's as bad as another to my way of thinkin'. But it seems that Chicago feller thinked dif'rent."

"It really was one of the very rare death's-head moths?" cried Nan, delighted.

"So he said. And he was willin' ter back up his belief with cold cash," declared Toby, smiting his leg for emphasis. "He paid us harnsome for it; and he said he'd take a lot more spec'mens if—

"Har! Here ye be, Hen," he added, breaking off to greet Nan's uncle. "I got suthin' to say to you. I kin say it now, for I ain't beholden ter nobody.

With what me and the ol' woman had scrimped and saved, an' what this feller from Chicago give Corson, I done paid off my debt to ol' Ged Raffer, an' the little farm's free and clear."

"I'm glad to hear it, Tobe," Uncle Henry declared, shaking hands with the old lumberman again. "I certain sure am glad to hear it! I'm pleased that you shouldn't have that worry on your mind any longer."

"And it has been a worry," said Old Toby, shaking his head. "More'n you think for. Ye see, it snarled me all up so's I warn't my own master."

"I see."

"Ye see, Ged was allus after me to go inter court an' back up his claim ag'in you on that Perkins Tract."

"I see," said Henry Sherwood again, nodding.

"On the other hand, you wanted me, if I knowed which was right, to witness, too. If I'd witnessed for Ged, ev'rybody wuld ha' thought I done it because he had a mortgage on the farm."

"I s'pose so," admitted Uncle Henry.

"Or, if I helped you, they'd ha' thought you'd bribed me—mebbe helped me git square with Ged."

"I couldn't. Too poor just now," said Uncle Henry, grimly. "But I'd the mind for it, Toby."

"Well, there ye be. Whichever way the cat jumped, I'd lost the respect of the community," said the old lumberman. "But now I am independent, I don't give a dern!"

Mr. Sherwood looked at him expectantly. Toby's "wizzled" face shone.

"I got a debt owin' to that leetle gal you got here, and somethin' to pay off to Tommy, too. But money won't do it, ef I had money. I am goin' to tell what I know about that boundary, though, Hen, and it will do YOU good! I can find another old feller, livin' down Pale Lick way, that can corroborate my evidence.

"You can git that injunction vacated at once, Hen, if you want, and put your axe-men right back into the Perkins Tract to work. That's what I come 'round to tell ye."

Aunt Kate was moved to tears, an unusual expression of emotion on her part. Being of pioneer stock, and having suffered much in the past, Nan's aunt was not easily moved. Uncle Henry was delighted. It was a great day for the Sherwoods.

It was another great day when, a week later, the roan ponies were brought to the door and Nan's trunk was strapped upon the back of the buckboard. Uncle Henry was to drive her to the train; but she would travel alone to Chicago to meet her chum, Bess Harley.

"And go to Lakeview Hall! I never did really expect I'd get there," Nan sighed, as she clung to Aunt Kate's neck. "It almost makes me forget that Momsey and Papa Sherwood are not at home yet.

"But, my dear!" she added, "if such a thing could be, you and Uncle Henry have taken the place of my own dear parents all these months I have been at Pine Camp. I've had a dee-lightful time. I'll never forget you all. I love you, love you, love you."

The roan ponies started on the jump. The boys cheered her from the corner of the house, having bashfully remained in the background. Even Margaret Llewellen and her impish brother, Bob, appeared and shrilly bade her goodbye.

Nan was off for school, and wonderful adventures lay before her!